i

AIN'T MUCH OF A WAR

*Reverent and Irreverent
Stories About the
Vietnam Conflict*

Frank Grzyb

Illustrated by
Alexandre V. Kouznetsov

Pocol Press

POCOL PRESS
Published in the United States of America
by Pocol Press
6023 Pocol Drive
Clifton, VA 20124
www.pocolpress.com

Publisher's Cataloguing-in-Publication

Grzyb, Frank

    Ain't much of a war / Frank Grzyb. – 1st ed. – Clifton, VA : Pocol Press, 2005.

    p. ; cm

    Collection of fictional tales about the Vietnamese Conflict.
    ISBN: 978-1-929763-22-1

    1.Vietnamese Conflict, 1961-1975—Fiction. 2. War stories. 3. Historical fiction. I. Title.

PS3557.R993 A655 2005
813.54—dc22   0505

Illustrations: Alexandre V. Kouznetsov
Cover photo: Frank Grzyb

"Medic! Medic!", "The Revelation According to Cabral", and "The Christmas Tree" first appeared in *Sensations Magazine*.

ACKNOWLEDGEMENTS

My heartfelt thanks is extended to Chris Duckworth and Tom Portelance for reading and critiquing, either à la carte or as an entrée, my manuscript. Their comments, advice, and words of encouragement proved invaluable.

Thanks also to Thanh Do Nguyen for providing the English to Vietnamese translations.

Without the assistance of Marguerite Beal, Donna Rubel, and Jodi Kennedy, my reputation as a computer neophyte would have remained unchallenged.

To Tom Hetrick at Pocol Press, a special thanks for believing in my work and all the helpful suggestions during the editorial process.

Bringing the stories within this book to life was masterfully achieved through the skillful hands of Alexandre Kouznetsov. Sasha's ideas are truly unique and his illustrations reflect his multi-faceted talents and passion as an artist.

To my wife, Ginny — a former high school English teacher of thirty-three years and now a college instructor — 'I couldn't have done it without you.'

Most importantly, rarely does a day go by when I'm not appreciative for all the borrowed time: to raise a family; to love and be loved; to enjoy my friends; and, to make new acquaintances, something many good men were never afforded. For this, and so much more, I'm deeply indebted to a far greater authority, a power even higher than the Chairman of the Joint Chiefs of Staff and the President.

DISCLAIMER

Also by Frank Grzyb: *Touched by the Dragon*
Released in trade paperback as
A Story for All Americans: Vietnam, Victims, and Veterans

AUTHOR'S NOTE

Years after my encounter with the dragon, I was asked by an inquisitive soul, "Would you be willing to relive the experience?" — the Vietnam experience, that is. The answer spewed from my lips like a long dormant but now active volcano: "No way!" I replied. Why the terse response considering I wasn't a foot soldier? Here's why. In Vietnam the enemy targeted every American whether cook or infantryman. Undoubtedly the odds of being wasted multiplied for a grunt, but because the conflict was a guerilla war, luck played a vital role in determining a soldier's ultimate fate regardless of military occupation. I was fortunate once. Today, I'm far less confident I'd survive a similar ordeal. Any lingering thoughts I entertained about my own invincibility vanished years ago. With age comes wisdom, perhaps even a heaping teaspoon of cowardice.

Most male, post-World War II baby-boomers growing up during the mid-to-late '60s and early '70s dreaded induction and the likelihood of going off to war. After all, how many were willing to risk their life defending a cause and a country they knew little if anything about? As I remember the times, this frightening thought mulled in my mind nearly every waking hour.

After receiving my draft notice, I visited an eye specialist who examined me for a minor abnormality — a scarred and blocked tear duct — a condition I had learned to cope with adequately since childhood. The doctor, knowing full well my tenuous situation, transcribed his findings in excruciating detail on a physician's notepad: Patient's right eye tears erratically causing blurred vision . . . susceptible to frequent infections, et cetera. I've nothing to substantiate my belief, but I always suspected he exaggerated the diagnosis making it appear more debilitating. Armed with the note along with Yankee ingenuity, I created a few fictitious ailments of my own and described them in dramatic detail to a military physician during a pre-induction physical. He wasn't moved or, for that matter, fooled. I suspect he heard the same suspicious tales of woe hundreds of times before. Within days, I was raising my right hand and swearing allegiance to my country.

No longer was I Frankie, son of Frank and Rose Grzyb, from the Podunk town I thought time had long since forgotten. Phew, was I ever mistaken. After receipt of a single letter with the overused, yet still haunting salutation, "Greetings," my personal identity was lost to a number. That's right . . . a number. Almost overnight, I ventured from worrying about financing graduate school to a more pressing concern: how would I, as US52958783, remain in one piece? There was something else that troubled me. My father saw five brothers off to war. From the first days of World War II and then in Korea where a cousin served, my family's legacy was cast in military concrete. Who was I to question the morality and righteousness of fighting in Vietnam or, even worse, breaking the family tradition of honorably serving our country in time of need?

Yes, I admit it. I watched, with nary a whimper, as my protective shield of naiveté slowly imploded — not a pleasurable experience as best I recollect.

A year after induction, I was ordered to Vietnam. During my tour, I was stationed alongside 250,000 other Americans scattered throughout the country. Thousands like me served in silent protest. Just do your time, don't make any trouble, and keep your head down, I kept telling myself. There were others with more intense feelings. Men felt betrayed by their own government, bitter about having to serve in what they believed, another country's civil war. They lived nearly every day of their tours under the thinly veiled cloak of righteous indignation.

Serving in Vietnam wasn't easy; yet being in the military did me good. Before then, my only excursion outside the continental United States was to Puerto Rico while on spring break from college. My concept of the world was seriously flawed. Some would argue, "It needn't take a war to bring the man out of the boy." For me it did. Living in a small community and nurtured by strict parents, I was sheltered from evil, although I did experience six years of parochial school, the first hint that all was not well in the world (the nuns threw blackboard erasers at me and smacked my knuckles with wooden yardsticks — all well deserved).

Vietnam hit me hard, as if leveled by an assault vehicle, yet it proved to be the catalyst I so desperately needed. My re-education — Reality 101 — commenced immediately. But it wasn't like anything I could ever have imagined. Combat played only a small role in my rehabilitation. It was the entire social and cultural experience, not only with the Vietnamese but also with those I was stationed alongside from the States, especially the inner-city kids. Within months, I learned more about life than my previous twenty-four years including six at college. When my tour ended, I was born anew and better prepared to conquer the world, the world of business, a jungle and hell in itself.

Am I proud to have served? I found little about the war to value, but my service to my country, as minuscule as it was, brings me immense pride even to this day. The final installment in this collection — "The Young Boy" — echoes this sentiment.

Over the years, I was fortunate to capture and retain an overabundance of ideas, putting them to pen only recently — "Medic . . . Medic!" and "The Crowning Glory" are two stories which immediately come to mind. "The Revelation According to Cabral" is another. Several other offerings are mental snapshots taken from actual events or loosely fabricated from tales I heard while in Vietnam. These are: "A Little Tail," "Dinner is Served," "Re-evaluating Newton's Law of Gravity," and "Lady."

"Esposito's Raid" is about an operation I wish I volunteered to lead. No such luck. Whether such an event happened is open to conjecture, but knowing the time and the place, I'd vote in the affirmative.

Few experiences in life are more difficult than being away from home during the holidays. Imagine for a moment celebrating the Yuletide season while stationed in a war zone thousands of miles away from family and friends. Believe me, it's devastating. A few months back, I stumbled upon a faded photograph in one of my old scrapbooks triggering a memory, which culminated in my writing

"The Christmas Tree." Looking at the faded snapshot, I was reminded of the only Christmas I ever spent away from home.

As for the remaining stories, all are a by-product of my overactive imagination and, some say, warped sense of humor.

DEDICATION

For Ginny, Matt, Katie, and Maria
My inspiration

TABLE OF CONTENTS

ILLUSTRATIONS

Never share a foxhole with someone
braver than yourself.

From *Murphy's Laws*
of Combat Operations

AIN'T MUCH OF A WAR

May your every wish be granted.
-Ancient Chinese Curse

The pilot of the Flying Tiger DC-9 no sooner taxied off the tarmac and shut down the engines when several olive-green buses pulled up to the passenger pick-up and drop-off area. Coming to a halt, the bus doors swung open and Marines disembarked. Private Lucas Teasdale was first to gather his gear.

"I can't wait to get out of here," said Teasdale. "'Nam can't be any worse than this stinkin' hole."

"Ya got that right," replied his buddy of six months, Private Sears.

"Soon, I'll be able to record me a kill," Teasdale boasted. "Those little, slant-eyed devils will be sorry they every tangled with this hombre."

Sears laughed. "Luke, I hope ya save a few for me?"

"Damn right, I will," Teasdale answered, offering a wry grin that contradicted his baby face expression. "Okinawa's been nothin' but misery: forced marches, candy-ass inspections, and guardin' empty warehouses. What a bunch of bullshit."

"It's crap all right," Sears replied. "Nothin' but unadulterated bull . . ."

"Shut your mouth, Marine!" Colonel Riley interjected, as he stepped from the passenger seat of a Jeep that led the entourage. Limping from the aftereffects of a wound he suffered during the Korean Conflict, Riley walked slowly, yet deliberately, to the front of the formation. Wasting little time, he delivered his brief remarks, "an appropriate sendoff speech" as he smugly called it:

1

The scheduled journey begins in an orderly fashion…

"Listen up, men. Where Uncle Sam's sending you . . . well . . . it ain't much of a war . . . but remember . . . it's the only one we have. Until someone finds a better one, you'll have to make do. Now go out there and kick ass like you've never kicked ass before. Ya got that?"

"Yeah . . . yeah!" the men cheered. There was no mistaking their confidence and youthful enthusiasm. For weeks, they were trained by the best, to be the best. They not only believed, but also had become, a uniform, invasive force not to be reckoned with by anyone.

As a refueling truck drove to the opposite side of the DC-9, a four-man detail pushed aluminum stairs against the passenger door facing the replacements. Within minutes, a stewardess opened the cabin door, secured it to the railing and walked back into the plane. Soon, men dressed in faded combat utilities and jungle boots stained creamy-orange from the scorching sun and dusty soil of Vietnam walked through the doorway. Slowly, they descended the stairs. Heads hung low as if unable to comprehend their change of environment. They carried nothing in their arms or on their backs, only dreadful memories in their hearts and souls. Fifteen months earlier, they had departed, as a unit, from the same airbase. Although most returned in a DC-9, some arrived earlier than expected in C-130's as cargo — corpses lying in dull-gray caskets with metal handles that rattled in cadence whenever the transport experienced turbulence.

As the men shuffled in single-file past the replacement battalion toward the empty buses, Sears gazed wide-eyed at his friend. Teasdale never looked up at Sears or the returning combat veterans. He did, however, hear a Marine say something to one of the replacements. The words disturbed him.

"Fresh meat, baby. You're nothin' but fresh meat."

Teasdale could have easily rubbed shoulders with any of the veterans. He chose not to. Staring at his jungle boots, all bright and shiny, he couldn't help but make a more subtle

...and ends with cold stares and silent voices.

assessment: Maybe this place wasn't that bad after all. Taking a deep breath, he reflected upon what his Dad and some of his uncles tried to tell him before he left for war. For the first time, Private Lucas Teasdale was beginning to realize there was more to soldiering than a macho attitude, tailored jungle fatigues, and the colorful unit patches that adorned them.

After the veterans boarded the buses and were driven away from the airfield, Colonel Riley addressed the replacements for a final time.

"All right, men. Let's load 'em up. Soon it'll be your turn to have some fun."

"MEDIC! MEDIC!"

...I've learned, the hard way, that some poems don't rhyme, and some stories
don't have a clear beginning, middle, and end.
-Gilda Radner, *It's Always Something* (1989)

"**R**ed! Red smoke!"
Willy's voice is difficult to hear above the roar of the turbine-driven engines and the slashing rotor blades. Yet, I can't help but listen as the peculiar instruments blend seamlessly into a hypnotic melody: *hummm . . . warp, warp, warp . . . hummm . . . warp, warp, warp. Funny*, I think: *Any other day, and I could be lulled to sleep.*

Whether Willy realizes it, I'm the only one who can hear him in the chopper. As the symphony of clashing metal continues, he persists with his warning:

"Red smoke! Red smoke! There's fuckin' gooks down there!"

Without warning, Willy punches my arm. Startled, I jerk my shoulder back. Realizing he has my undivided attention, Willy points toward the small rectangular window, an area no larger than a portable TV.

"Look . . . look!" he shouts.

I lean forward, peer outside, and see the smoke. I acknowledge his concern by nodding my head a few times.

To my right sits Riggs. Where we're sitting, billowing clouds of smoke are visible from the machine gunner's door. "Sonnava bitch!" Riggs mutters. "Damn!" he says, pulling on the chinstrap of his helmet. If he tightens it any more, he'll choke himself to death, I think: *Hell. Suicide may be a better option.* I smirk at my sick joke, but the enjoyment is short-lived.

Directly in front of me, Paul is praying: "Our Father . . . hallowed be thy name . . . forgive us our trespasses . . . and deliver us from evil. Amen!" I watch as he completes his abbreviated prayer by making a ritualistic Sign of the Cross, not once but three times, as if the rapid repetition will provide him more protection by

6

the Almighty. Paul's a Fuckin' New Guy. To me, the fright in Paul's eyes confirms his frail disposition and less than enviable status as an FNG.

While staring out the chopper door, my mind wonders: *What'm I doin' out here in this God-damned wasteland messin' with these gooks?* The thought isn't novel. I suspect hundreds of GIs scattered throughout the country have asked the same question. But to me, there's an irony. Strangely, I'm curious almost to the point of paranoia how I'll react in combat. During previous missions, I carved out a commendable record; but there's no cold, hard rule that states the same bravado will apply during successive encounters — once a hero, always a hero only has relevance in the movies.

It's bizarre how the mind processes data. Suddenly, I'm reminded of a Beatles song: Nowhere Man. Bastardizing the lyrics, I say to myself: *Here I am, a genuine nowhere man, fighting in a nowhere land, with no plans except my own survival.* Last night, my only desire was finding the time to gulp down a few warm beers and bullshit with the guys. Today, I have a far different concern: trying to stay alive.

Willy, Riggs, Paul and myself (the guys call me Doc), and about 25 others, find ourselves smack-dab in the middle of another in a long series of gut-wrenching missions. The foreboding sense of doom that is difficult, if not impossible, to shake, is lurking behind every thought. I'm confused. There's little good left to think.

Within minutes our unit — Delta Company — will be dropped into another hot Landing Zone (LZ). Our orders are dreadfully explicit: conduct a search and clear operation. The search ended before we landed. We would be responsible for the second phase. The lead chopper, Alpha Force Two Zero, landed earlier, and their reception was rather chaotic. From what we could ascertain listening to the radio transmission, bullets were ripping through the fuselage even before they landed. Men must have been killed where they sat. Despite the turmoil, the pilot managed to take off. Flying back to base camp, he radioed our chopper again:

"Eagle One, Eagle One, Alpha Force Two Zero, over."

7

"This is Eagle One. Go ahead Alpha Force Two Zero."

"Roger. The LZ is hot. Repeat, the LZ is hot. We took heavy small arms fire from the tree line to the south, and we have casualties. Drop your load and get the hell out of there."

"Roger, Alpha Force Two Zero. Read you loud and clear."

Meanwhile, a kid we call Weasel is taken ill. Several others follow suit, but not nearly as bad as Weasel. Hell. To me, he always seemed a bit anemic. I don't think he weighs more than 110 pounds, soaking wet. At 5' 4", I'm convinced; his nickname's appropriate. Now slumped and kneeling, he regurgitates what little remains in his stomach. A galvanized pail, strategically positioned on the deck plate, captures the contents of his queasy stomach. After awhile, Weasel gets the dry-heaves. I look over and sympathize with his plight. His condition reminds me of my own drinking days in high school and the, all-too-familiar scenario. Phlegm dangles from his mouth. He wipes it away, using the shirtsleeve of his jungle fatigues. Oddly, I feel no revulsion. Weasel's condition has nothing to do with airsickness or his previous dietary intake: booze and C-rations. His is nothing more than a nervous stomach. Although 25 of us are in the chopper, only a few notice Weasel's distress. Feeling incredibly alone, I suspect all our thoughts are strikingly similar: Will today be the day I die?

Combat is an indescribable horror made even worse by the type of war we've been forced to fight. Understand. The rules of engagement and the restrictions placed upon us make little, if any, sense. We've been ordered to ask questions first before pulling the trigger. The questionable and convoluted logic works something like this: *Excuse me, Sir! You're armed and walking in a restricted area. Are you the enemy? You are! Well, don't move a damn inch. I need approval from my superiors before I can waste you. Sir? Sir? Please come back. It'll only take a minute.*

Soon the situation will worsen, I know it will, but I do all humanly possible to refrain from thinking about the inevitable. Yet, even before the bullets fly, adrenaline is furiously pumping through my bloodstream. My heart is pounding. Sounding more like an automobile traveling on a bumpy road, *thump . . . thump . . .*

thump, than gentle waves washing against the seashore; if I didn't know better, I'd swear my ribcage is about to explode. Drawing a few deep breaths of stale, humid air, I try as a trained Yoga to slow its pace. My effort fails. If anything, it skips a beat.

"God, this shits!" I exclaim, not realizing I'm speaking out loud. It makes no difference; nobody hears me. Even if they had, they wouldn't have cared. All are too busy worrying about their own fragile existence.

About now, I'm scared, real scared. I make every effort to look busy by inventorying all my medical supplies. It helps. I do my usual check making sure my bandages and packing are tightly secured to my web belts (feminine sanitary napkins, I call them, because that's what they look like). Next, I double-check to make certain I carry hypodermic needles of morphine. *All set.* Although I know the three canteens of water I'm carrying are full, I inspect them again.

Why they made me a medic, I'll never know. Maybe they figured if they gave me a rifle, I'd shoot myself or someone else. They may have been right.

Deep in my gut, I have this feeling, and the co-pilot's radio message from Alpha Force Two Zero only serves to reinforce my concern. Within seconds, we'll be on the ground. Shit!

Pitched slightly aft and flying into the valley at a high rate of speed, our Chinook swoops down like a falcon, claws (wheels) extended as if preparing to capture its prey. In its wake, our chopper trails translucent streaks of blue mist as the pilot's rate of descent borders on the absurd. The wheels never touch down. Four to five feet above the ground, we're ordered to jump. Everyone except me is wearing a full complement of combat gear. The drop-zone is no larger than the circumference of a municipal cul-de-sac. Clusters of trees and, farther in, triple-canopy jungle surround the area. Each soldier is holding a weapon — an M16A1 5.56mm rifle, an M79 40mm grenade launcher, or an M60 7.62mm machine-gun. I'm loaded down with medical supplies.

"Get the hell out!" screams the door gunner.

Door gunners are self-confessed lunatics. Most see action nearly every mission and relish the opportunity to put their lives on the line. Some thrill. Although this guy may have been crazy, he wasn't stupid. The area is too hot even for his diet of living on the edge.

Bullets ricochet off the top of the fuselage above our heads, and the door gunner wants out.

"Move, you sons-a-bitches! Jump, God damn it, jump!" he yells, while spraying rounds from his machine-gun into the dense foliage directly ahead.

After the last man hits the ground the pilot jerks back on the control stick and maneuvers the chopper slightly to the left, swinging the large bird around nearly 180 degrees and speeds off in the same direction from which he came. I glance up and feel emptiness. *Remember what you're trained to do*, I repeat over and over in my head, all the while trying to appear as the consummate professional. Then, suddenly, I hear someone yelling:

"Doc! Over here."

I know it's Lieutenant Crandall, but I haven't a clue which way to turn.

"Where the hell are you?" I yell back, eager to obtain a general bearing on his position.

He calls out again. "I'm over here. Hurry up, Doc. For Christ sake, get over here."

Finally, I figure out his position. "I'm comin'. I'm comin'," I say.

Suddenly, a burst of machine-gun fire brings me back to reality as the bullets whiz over my head. Frozen and scared shitless, I make myself small by planting my face, chest, crotch, and legs firmly against the damp ground. It's the third time I've been shot at, at least directly, and each time is more frightening than the last. Kissing the ground is no longer a grunt's term with which I'm unfamiliar. My knees are knocking, and my bowels are about to burst.

"Doc!" the lieutenant screams, this time in anger. "If we don't make it to the tree line, we're all dead meat."

"I'm comin'!" I yell back.

Getting to my elbows and knees, I crawl as they taught me in basic training. Soon, I'm lying on my side next to the lieutenant. Small arms fire starts to intensify. Grunts direct their fire into the bushes directly ahead. Make no mistake. I did say bushes. The enemy is invisible, stealthily blending in with the jungle undergrowth. I say to myself, *This isn't what I had in mind.* Seeing too many combat movies as a kid at Saturday matinees had distorted my perception of reality. Nobody in his right mind, the enemy included, is going to allow himself to become an open target.

"It's about time, Doc," the lieutenant states almost in disgust. "Now stay with me until you're needed. Understand?"

"Yes, Sir! Yes, Sir!" I reply. Hell. I hadn't a clue what else to do.

Delta Company is scattered throughout the razor-sharp elephant grass. Not wasting any more time, Lieutenant Crandall rises to his knees to rally his men.

"Work your way over to that clump of trees to the north," he yells, before dropping to a prone position. Turning toward me, he says, "Follow me, Doc."

Slowly, we crawl toward the tree line approximately 50 yards away. For me, it's a marathon, but even worse, this endurance test is being accomplished on hands and knees. Suddenly, out of nowhere, a burst of machine-gun fire rips into the grass directly ahead. *Rat-tat-tat. Rat-tat-tat. Rat-tat-tat.* The enemy is relentless. I remain prone, waiting for the terror to end as bullets hit all around. Suddenly, a round finds its mark: me. Stunned, I feel no pain. *Why is there no pain? Am I dead?* Not knowing what else to do, I move my hand toward the area and pull it back to eye level as I search for blood. There is none. I look down and see that a round had ripped through one of my canteens before exiting through another, splattering water all over my lower fatigue jacket and pants, perhaps mixing with urine from my kidneys that I'm no longer able to control.

"Medic! Medic!" screams a wounded GI.

Although the voice is unrecognizable, I see a soldier bobbing up and down about thirty yards to my right, further away from the tree line than I would have liked. Gunfire erupts again. I don't see or hear him again, but I see his figure long enough to pinpoint his approximate location.

Lieutenant Crandall and I look at each other. "Good luck, Doc," he says. Nothing else is spoken.

Methodically, I crawl in the direction where I'd last seen the soldier. After slithering on the ground like a snake for more than a minute, I come upon two men.

"Doc!" a highly agitated private says to me. I recognize him as Paul St. Laurent, the new guy in our company. Nobody knows much about him.

"Riggs's been hit!"

"Where?" I ask.

"In his arm," Paul says.

"Move over and let me see. How you doin', Riggs?" I ask.

"It hurts bad, Doc, real bad," as he writhes in pain.

"I know," I say. It's his left forearm. "It's not that bad, Riggs."

I attempt to reassure him, knowing he's not the strongest of individuals when it comes to pain (Once, back at base camp, I removed a splinter from his finger. You would have thought it was major surgery). He knows I'm lying. My face can't hide my concerned expression. The muscle is dangling and a large bone is exposed. Immediately, I give him an injection of morphine and tie a tourniquet around his upper arm.

"This'll help," I tell him.

"Thanks, Doc," he says, gritting his teeth. He cries a little. The tears leave irregular streaks in the dirt on his face.

Within seconds, the drug takes effect, and he quiets down. With the only canteen that remains intact, I pour water around his forearm, being careful not to spill any into the wound. The last thing I need is to treat an infection. Next, I rip a bandage from my web belt, open the package and wrap the bandage around his arm. There isn't enough. I need a second. Just as I finish dressing the wound, another burst of machine-gun fire hits our area. I roll on top of Riggs. When the firing subsides, I push myself off his chest.

"You all right, Riggs?"

"I don't know, Doc. My arm's still pretty bad."

"How 'bout you?" I ask turning toward St. Laurent. He remains face down on the ground. Quickly, I crawl a few feet over to where he's lying. "Paul, Paul . . . are you all right?" There's no response. Slowly, I roll him over onto his side. His forehead is a mess, almost like it exploded. One of his eyes is shut; the other dangles from its socket and lies on his cheek. *A round must have hit him in the back of the head*, I think. As terrible as he looks, I check for vital signs: no pulse, no breathing. Nothing. St. Laurent, a guy I hardly knew, is my first combat fatality.

Regaining my senses, I crawl the short distance over to Riggs. "We've gotta get the hell out of here," I say in earnest.

"What about Paul?"

"There's nothin' we can do for him. Now listen. We've gotta make it to those trees." I point over his shoulder. "We've gotta get up and make a run for it. I'll support you. Can you do it?"

"I don't know, Doc. How 'bout Paul . . ."

"Forget about Paul," I interject. "He's dead. There's nothing we can do for him."

"But my arm, Doc."

"You candy-ass," I say. "It's not that bad." I look him in the eye and say, "Ya wanna make a run for it, or do we die right here?"

I had to motivate him and shaming him seemed my only option. After all, even a wimp gets pissed once in a while. Besides, I wasn't kidding. If we make a run for it, we've got a chance; stay here and we're goners.

"What do ya want me to do?" he asks, as he gathers up an infinitesimal dose of courage.

It worked. "Okay then. When I say 'go,' I want ya to pull yourself up and start runnin' toward the trees. I'll be right beside you. Ya got it?"

"Ya, I got it," he says.

"Okay . . . let's go, Go, GO!"

Riggs and I are on our feet in an instant, running toward the trees. When the gooks spot us, they concentrate their small arms fire in our direction. No more than 20 yards from the tree line, Riggs stumbles, taking me down with him.

Weasel, who had made it to safety, sees what's happening. Immediately, he jumps from behind a tree and makes a mad dash toward our position. The machine-gun opens up again; only this time I hear loud explosions in the distance. *Boom. Boom.* A couple of our men, probably from the first assault chopper, find the machine-gun nest and are close enough to throw hand grenades. The explosions continue. *Boom . . . boom . . . boom.* The machine-gun is silenced, yet enemy small arms fire continues.

Seemingly from nowhere, Weasel dives into the elephant grass and slides into the back of my boots, startling me for an instant. Crawling a few feet to my side and before catching his breath, he asks, "Need . . . some . . . help?"

"Hell, yes! We've got to get Riggs behind the tree line." I point in the direction we must navigate. "We don't have far to go. Ya game?" I ask.

"Sure am, Doc."

"Great," I say.

"But how 'bout him?" Weasel asks. No sooner do the words leave his lips then he understands. "Holy shit!" he blurts out, "It's the fuckin' new guy!"

"He's dead, Weasel. Don't worry about him. We'll get his body later," I say. How he recognizes the lifeless body as St. Laurent defies reason. There aren't many features intact to distinguish a face.

Suddenly, Riggs cries out, "Get me outta here! Please, for God sake, get me outta here!"

"Let's go, guys!" I yell. Weasel is the first to jump to his feet, pulling Riggs along with him.

Pushing myself up, I grab Riggs under his bad arm and secure him by his waist. All three of us run the best we can toward the tree line. Riggs stumbles, momentarily, causing Weasel and me to lose stride.

"Faster . . . faster!" Weasel yells. Rounds are hitting all around. A rush of adrenaline shoots through my body.

Only seven or eight more strides, I say to myself. Suddenly, Weasel collapses. His entire body twists and lurches backward; his left arm flails in the air before hitting the ground. The momentum pulls Riggs and me down with him. At first, I think he stumbled, but then it dawns on me, although I don't want to believe it.

"Weasel!" I scream. "Get up!"

Weasel is lying on his back his face turned toward me. His fatigue shirt is saturated in blood. Worse, I notice blood trickling from his mouth, nose, and ears. *Shit, man! Not Weasel*! I'm losing it, yet I know I can't. Quickly, I regain my composure. While ripping off Weasel's shirt, he groans and coughs up blood. He's having breathing difficulties. Without reason, I stare at this huge gaping wound in his back and left shoulder, bigger than I've ever seen before on a human being, even a dead gook.

"Damn," I mumble under my breath. "Hang in there, Weasel, you'll be okay," I say out loud.

Riggs, lying beside me, starts to cry. "Help me, Doc! Help me! Don't let me die! Please don't let me die!"

"For Christ's sake, Riggs. You're not gonna die!" I say. "Weasel's hurtin' real bad. I've gotta take care of him first." Riggs simply turns away.

Lieutenant Crandall and Willy, seeing what is happening, crawl over to help.

"Doc, what do you want us to do?" the Lieutenant asks.

"Take Riggs to the trees," I tell him. "I've gotta take care of Weasel. Until the bleeding stops, he can't be moved."

The lieutenant looks at Willy, who has just arrived, and immediately gives him an order: "Get him up and out of here. I'm staying to help, Doc."

Willy grunts and moves his head to signify his readiness. Moments later, he and Riggs are on their feet. Their dash is short. Both make it to safe cover.

"Lieutenant," I say. "Help me roll him over." Lieutenant Crandall pulls Weasel by the hips as I gently guide him by his uninjured shoulder. Weasel's fatigues resemble rags. Quickly, I tear the rest of his shirt away. Weasel's breathing is shallow. Staring down, I notice a small bullet hole in his chest wall directly above his left nipple. "Shit!" I holler.

"What's wrong?" asks the lieutenant.

"He's got a sucking chest wound," I say.

The small entry wound bubbles like a bottle of seltzer water. With nothing restricting the flow, air is freely passing through the hole. Suddenly, my medical training kicks in, not to mention my adrenalin. Weasel's lung has collapsed. If left unchecked, he's dead in a matter of minutes. I need to cover the hole with something other than my hand, and I know it has to be impermeable material, something like a plastic bag. Obviously plastic bags are difficult to find in a jungle, so I do the next best thing. "Lieutenant!" I say.

"What, Doc?"

"Pull out the pack of cigarettes in my shirt pocket."

"Which pocket?" he asks.

"This one," I reply, as I position the pocket toward him.

He sticks his hand in and pulls out the cigarettes. With a quizzical look, he asks, "Now what?"

"Pull off the tab and give me the cellophane wrapper."

He does as I request and hands it to me. Removing my hand from the chest wound, I wipe away the excess blood and place the wrapper over the hole. Within seconds, Weasel's breathing seems less labored, though far from normal.

"Take a bandage off my belt," I tell the lieutenant.

"Here." He hands it to me.

Taking the bandage, I place it over the wrapper as tightly as possible, being careful not to break the seal of the cellophane covering the wound. I wrap the tapered ends around his back and tie them in a knot. "Now, Lieutenant. Help me pull him onto his side."

"Okay," he says. Together, we roll him over, taking considerable care to prevent further injury.

I can't get over the size of the wound in Weasel's back. For a moment, I experience a morbid fascination. Looking at it is surreal.

I think, *It just can't be true . . . but it is*. Improbable as it is, I'm witnessing firsthand that a person can lose that much skin, muscle, and blood and still be alive. Lieutenant Crandall nearly pukes. He turns away. Methodically, I pull out all the gauze packing from my web belt, rip off the wrapping and stuff them in the gaping wound. Weasel groans. To me, that's a good sign. He's still alive. Soon, I run out of packing.

"Lieutenant! Give me your packing and bandages, and make it quick," I command.

No longer are we following military protocol. He's become my assistant, and a good one at that. Using what he gives me, I pack the wound, and then tightly wrap the gauze around Weasel's chest and shoulder.

"Now what?" Lieutenant Crandall asks.

"We can't move him," I say, as I inject Weasel with a shot of morphine. "I'm afraid the bleeding will start again. I'll stay with him. We've got to get him tied to an IV and medevac'd the hell out of here."

Lieutenant Crandall looks at me and understands the urgency.

"I'm going back to the RTO and call for a dust-off."

Picking himself up, he makes a mad dash toward his men, drawing a few rounds of fire.

Weasel starts to shake. I can tell he's going into shock. Perhaps I should have waited with the morphine. It's too late, I tell myself. Lying on the ground, I roll out of my fatigue jacket and place it over his chest. Despite the jungle heat and humidity, he's got the chills.

"You'll be all right, Weasel. I've got you patched up real good. A chopper's on its way."

Taking off my canteen, I pour water on my handkerchief and wipe the blood from his face. Weasel groans again. Whether he's thanking me for my kindness or reacting to the excruciating pain, I'll never know. I suspect it's the latter.

From head to toe, I'm bathed in blood, first Riggs', then Paul's. Now it's Weasel's turn to darken the color of my sun-faded fatigues. With the little water that remains in my canteen, I pour

17

some on my hands and wipe them on my pants. I do it a second time, as the first wash seems ineffective. Looking down, I realize that my palms are bleeding profusely, not because of injuries inflicted by the enemy, but from the razor sharp elephant grass I've been crawling around in for almost an hour. But there's little time to worry about my minor abrasions; Weasel's dying.

"Hang in there, Buddy, hang in there. I hear the choppers comin'," I whisper in his ear.

But, I lie. Where the hell are they? What's taking them so long? By the time the firing ceases and the first bird flies over, it's too late. Weasel dies in my arms, just as the lead chopper sets down in the clearing. Carefully, I roll his lifeless body on the ground, first his back, then his head. Leaning over, I slide my fatigue jacket off his chest and over his face. There's no way I want to make eye contact. With shoulders slumped, I lean back on my calves and reflect: *But there wasn't anything I could do . . . nothing . . . not a goddamned thing.* Lowering my face, I cry in a muffled whimper: "Why, God? Why?"

I feel faint and a little sick to my stomach as beads of sweat roll down my brow. After wiping away the perspiration, I sit down and light a cigarette. Looking at my hands, I notice they are no longer bloodied. All I see are scars, fine-lined, as if cut with surgical precision and left to heal without first-aid.

Unexpectedly, I hear footsteps from behind, but before I can turn to see who it is, I'm startled by a voice.

"Gary, Gary!"

"What?" I ask as if rudely awakened from a sound sleep.

"Honey. It's Ellen. Are you okay?" she asks, while gently touching my shoulder.

I shudder for a second and then respond: "I'm all right," as I pull out a handkerchief from my pants pocket to wipe, what now has become, a deluge of sweat running down my brow. "I'm a bit hot," I tell her. "I must have turned the thermostat up too high when I got out of bed this morning." Whether the victim of a flashback or a hallucinogenic trance, I can't be sure, but of one fact I'm certain: I'd give anything to avoid a repeat performance.

Ellen continues to question me. "Wow! I've never seen you so intense. Are you sure you're all right? You're all flushed and sweaty."

"I'm fine, Ellen," I say, as I masquerade my recovery. Impulsively, I stand up, lean forward, pull her against my chest and give her an enormous hug.

"What's that for?" she asks, perplexed by my surprising display of affection.

"It just feels good to be alive today, Baby!"

"But it's raining outside."

"Makes no matter, Ellen. Trust me."

"Whatever you say, Gary." She gives me one of those funny stares only a wife can extend, then walks away to pour a cup of coffee.

For the moment, my thoughts revolve around the men we lost in Vietnam so many years ago; those I still remember and others whose names I've long since forgotten. *It never gets easier*, I think. I let out a sigh, as much in relief as frustration.

After placing her coffee cup on the table, Ellen comes up from behind and wraps her arms around my shoulders. "What say we take a ride to Hyannis, shop a bit, then have dinner at *The Black Cat*? The traffic shouldn't be bad, and the weather's supposed to clear before noon."

"Okay," I say. "Just give me twenty minutes to shave and shower." Ellen knows something isn't right. Call it a wife's intuition. She learned over our thirty years of marriage not to push particular issues.

Like most men, I find shopping outranks little on my priority list, barely surpassing my bi-annual visit to the proctologist, whom I always suspected to be a direct descendent of Marquis de Sade. Yet (don't quote me on this), I actually enjoy watching Ellen in a feeding frenzy, hunting for, what she calls, bargains. Over the years, I've learned, 'When she's happy, I'm happy.'

Ellen also knows my major weakness. Rarely do I pass up an opportunity for a chilled martini with a twist of lemon peal, and those at *The Black Cat* are nothing less than exquisite; "shaken, not stirred" as Ian Fleming's James Bond prefers.

But, before I partake of libations, I promise, I'll do as always. In silence, and unbeknownst to Ellen, I'll toast the likes of Paul and Weasel, memories of men that remain as fresh today as the day I last saw them alive.

The End of a Bad Dream

ESPOSITO'S RAID

Our problems are man-made, therefore they may be solved by man ...
No problem of human destiny is beyond human beings.
-John F. Kennedy, Address, American University (June 10, 1963)

"You stupid, pea-brained imbecile!" screamed Sergeant Esposito.

Along with his voice, Esposito's expression was nothing short of unbridled fury: bulging eyes, fiery-red cheeks, wrinkled forehead lines, and a mouth opened so wide that if someone didn't know better, they'd swear he was about to spit venom. Berserk with anger, he continued to spew a profuse litany of obscenities. Nobody dared to interrupt. Frankly, a rabid dog seemed far less menacing.

"Who . . . I repeat . . . who the fuck told you to take a prisoner?" as he pointed toward the blindfolded, gagged, and bound figure quivering in the corner of the dimly lit room.

Mercilessly, Sgt. Esposito continued to lambaste PFC Canty with his vulgar barrage until the soldier's self-worth was reduced to smoldering rubble. Although Esposito's disposition rivaled a fire-breathing dragon, never once did he slip and reveal any of their true identities. Somehow, he managed at least a shred of self-control.

Although Canty's head was lowered, it was cocked far enough back to allow him a full view of Esposito's every move. Suffering through the outburst for what seemed like an eternity, Canty mustered enough courage to break into, what to then had been, a one-sided conversation. Speaking softly at first, he tried to gain the sergeant's attention.

"Sarge . . . Sarge!" When no response was forthcoming, he tried again, only this time with more determination: "Sarge . . . Sarge. Listen to me!"

"What, for Christ's sake?" cried Esposito, looking none too pleased by the interruption.

22

"I'm sorry, Sarge . . . really I am. I dunno why I did what I did."

Esposito's face reddened even more than before as he erupted: "You don't know why?" all the while shaking his head in disbelief. "For Christ's sake, man, a God damned six year old woulda known better!"

PFC Sylvester Canty barely masqueraded as a soldier in the United States Army. Short and stocky, Canty was noticeably overweight by army standards — actually, he was considerably overweight by any medical standard, civilian or military. His mental faculties were even more suspect. Canty was fortunate to have graduated from high school. Rumors circulated throughout the compound that school administrators pushed him out the door awarding him a diploma despite his intellectual shortcomings just because he was a likable, though, mindless scholar.

"Now what are we supposed to do?" Esposito quizzed. "Taking prisoners was not, I repeat, was not an option," raising his voice to accentuate his distain.

Nobody answered.

"Jesus Christ! How much simpler could this have been . . . and you had to go screw it all up, God damn it!" While pacing the floor, Esposito momentarily took his eyes off Canty transferring his stare to SPC4 Carl Zalinski. "Man, I shoulda' never listened to you in the first place!" he snapped.

Within seconds Esposito was back peering at Canty, shoveling more verbal diarrhea his way.

"You're nothin' but an enormous screw-up, you know that don't you?"

By now, Canty's mind was spinning like a whirlwind. There wasn't anyone who doubted the private's guilt, but in an inexplicable way, many sympathized with his genetic shortcomings. To them, Canty was as much a victim as the villain.

Zalinski watched what was happening until he thought it wise to intercede on behalf of his friend. It was evident that the sniveling private needed all the help he could muster.

"Sarge! I'm the one at fault, not that poor bastard," Zalinski said as he gazed at the slumped-shouldered private "I shoulda kept a . . ." But before he could finish, he was interrupted.

"But you didn't, and now we're all in a heap of shit," Esposito interjected.

It didn't take Zalinski long to realize that his defensive maneuver was futile. Esposito had no intention of listening to reason, or at the very least, relinquishing the floor.

By now, Canty was overwhelmed and mentally drained of any thoughts normally expected of a rational human being. Everyone who witnessed the unfolding events realized, if they hadn't before, that even an amoeba possessed more wits than did the Private. As an occasional tear ran down his cheeks, Canty again asked for forgiveness.

"I'm sorry, really I am, Sarge. I just screwed up," as he lowered his head like a sad puppy-dog that he resembled. "I don't know what happened . . . please forgive me. I just got carried away . . . yeah, carried away, that's what happened!"

"Carried away? That's what you call it?" mumbled Esposito under his breath as he began to pace the floor a second time. During his walk, he bumped into the shoulder of one of the men standing in the cramped quarters of the wooden barracks, but he was too immersed in his own thoughts to be concerned with the obtrusion or to offer a polite, "Excuse me." The narrow room was the same operations center where the raid was initially planned and would have concluded had it not been for Sylvester's monumental screw-up.

"Look!" Esposito said. "All the bitchin' in the world ain't gonna' help. I've got to think this through. I've got to figure out somethin' damn quick," and as if pained to say it, "or . . . all our asses will be in a sling, especially mine." Although Esposito regained his senses, almost immediately, he lapsed into an irrational tirade. "Christ sakes! How do I explain this to the Sergeant Major? Damn? He's gonna tear me a new asshole for sure."

"I'm sorry, Sarge!" Canty cried out, with even more heartfelt emotion. The tears flowed freely as he sobbed into his cupped hands.

Esposito lifted his head. For the first time since he lit into Canty, he knew he had gone too far. "Ahhh shit!" he muttered, brushing his short hair back with his hand while holding his baseball-style, fatigue hat in the other. Looking directly at the PFC, he said, "Listen to me, man! We'll figure somethin' out. It's not that bad. Now go sit over there and pull yourself together," as he pointed toward an empty bunk in the far corner of the room.

Esposito was well aware of the seriousness of his dilemma. What started out as a brilliantly conceived plan had now degenerated into a seriously flawed mission. The possibility of punishment now appeared inevitable.

Esposito was at a loss. "Any of you guys got any bright ideas?" he asked. "I sure as hell don't."

Subversive operations and clandestine maneuvers were commonplace throughout Vietnam. No surprise here. But the mission Esposito methodically designed was noticeably different than all the others. Whether American soldiers at war ever conducted similar raids are open to conjecture, but one fact remained certain: this operation was extremely unusual, not to mention highly controversial.

Planning for the raid had taken weeks. Designed as a hit and run operation, it was to be both cunning and swift. Failure was never considered and nothing was left to chance. Sgt. Esposito made that clear from the start. The mission was Esposito's sole inspiration and responsibility from inception. Should it fail, he'd be the one held accountable. He needed no reminder. Although a heavy burden, he accepted the enormous challenge as part of his destiny.

Just how important was the operation, and how would it be recorded in the annals of military history? In no way, shape or form would the event have even the slightest impact upon the outcome of the war. There would be no legacy, not even an award.

Did the raid have a strategic purpose? Yes, it did, but in a perverse sort of way. The operation revolved around a strategic area and the securing of what best could be described as forbidden contraband.

Each man had been hand-selected by Esposito, Canty being the only exception. Although Zalinski had recommended Canty, Esposito had deep reservations. Canty's reputation as a screw-up had preceded him, although Zalinski continued to insist that the criticism was unwarranted.

"Don't worry, Sarge. He'll be with me all the time. I'll keep an eye on him," Zalinski promised. It was a promise he'd soon come to regret.

Esposito relented, but not before telling the specialist that he held him responsible "should Canty step on his crank or anyone else's."

Esposito had been explaining the operation to the men for over an hour. "Now that you understand the mission, let's go out there and make yourself proud." Thinking for a second he added, "And whatever you do, don't let your sorry asses get caught. You hear me?"

There was a scattering of "yeah's" from the men.

Esposito wasn't satisfied with the response. "What did you say?"

"Yeaaah!" hollered the men in near-perfect unison.

"That's better!" he said.

Esposito continued. "Except for Pasquale, you'll work in teams of two. "Each area will prove a challenge. Oh yeah! Before I forget. There'll be guards to bribe. Remember that! And, also, find out who's on guard duty tomorrow night and pay them off with a few packs of cigarettes the first chance you get."

Just when everyone thought Esposito was finished, he barked our even more commands. "Remember. No weapons. We don't want casualties, either our side or theirs. As for the time, you've got only an hour. If it takes you any longer, you're doing something you shouldn't be doing," as a smirk appeared on his face. "Remember . . . no weapons. And one last bit of advice; keep your mouths shut. We don't need anyone being ID'd."

"Okay, men," Esposito said in closing. "We'll meet back here tomorrow . . . say about midnight. Are there any questions?"

"What are we gonna do with all the stuff we bring back?" asked SPC4 Roy Zimmerman.

"You'll see," said Esposito breaking into a sly grin. "That'll be my job. But you can bet your ass about one thing; it'll be put to good use."

"Anyone else?" Esposito asked again. "No . . . okay! Let's call it a night. Remember. Don't be late. See you tomorrow."

The day of reckoning was at hand. The time: roughly 20 minutes before midnight.

First to enter Esposito's room — now a makeshift command and control center — was CPL Dominic Pasquale, a street-wise kid from northern New Jersey. Pasquale came from a congested borough infamously known for its overabundance of trailer trucks and distribution warehouses, not to mention a high crime rate. His city was as much a 'concrete jungle' as Manhattan. Like so many other kids trying to survive, Pasquale became a numbers runner before he turned fourteen. Only days after his sixteenth birthday, he was arrested for larceny — the charge: grand theft auto. Because it was his first offense, the judge was lenient. Pasquale got a slap on the wrist: a suspended sentence. Since then, he managed to keep his record clean, though he toyed with the legal system on several occasions. The police just couldn't finger him for a crime. Try as they may, there was never enough evidence for an arrest, never mind a conviction. Pasquale was coy and oh so smooth.

Esposito greeted the corporal the same way he would the others. "Are you man enough to accept this assignment?"

"Damn right!" Pasquale responded. Pasquale had, as they say, 'been there and done that.' Compared to all his previous assignments in Vietnam, this mission would be a cakewalk, at least as far as he was concerned.

Minutes later, Zimmerman and Zalinski strolled in. Zimmerman was originally from White Plains, New York. Zalinski was from Warren, Michigan. His idea of a night out on the town was driving downtown to Detroit and raising hell. Until he was drafted, he had never been outside his home state.

Viera was the next to arrive. SPC4 Russell Viera was a rich kid from Redwood, California. Nobody in the company was sure where the family money came from. Perhaps nobody thought to ask. All they knew, Viera sported a thick bankroll and made no qualms about spending it on his buddies and himself at the Enlisted Men's Club.

As was his usual modus operandi, PFC Sylvester Canty was the last to arrive. "Better late than never, huh, Sarge?" he said.

Esposito wasn't pleased but held his tongue. Canty came from Wilkes-Barre, Pennsylvania. Prior to the military, he worked briefly in the steel mills before enlisting for a four-year hitch in the army. He was a big, slobbering kind of a guy, standing six feet tall and weighing in at about 240 pounds — down 25 pounds since he first enlisted. Looking at Canty many could say he was better suited for a pie eating contest than a tour of duty in 'Nam. Being wartime, the army wasn't too selective nor did they shape him into a man as the recruiting posters advertised.

Strangely enough, the units taking part in the mission were support personnel from the 240th Quartermaster Battalion, reinforced by members of the 599th Personnel Services Company. The combat support group operated under the 1st Logistics Command (the design of the shoulder patch worn by the men — a broad, red arrow slanted at a 45-degree angle on a field of blue — was called the Leaning Shithouse because that is what it resembled). The command was located on the outskirts of the coastal city of Qui Nhon, a fishing community with over 175,000 inhabitants.

Twenty minutes past midnight, Esposito made the final assignments. "Zalinski. You and Canty raid the village. Zimmerman, you and Viera will operate near the hospital." Neither team had to go very far. The hospital was at the southern end of the compound. Esposito continued. "And you, Pasquale, will be responsible for the small, concrete building adjacent the hospital."

"Any questions?" Esposito asked.

"What if the guards don't let us pass?" asked Viera.

"Didn't you take care of that this morning?"

"Yeah, we did," Zimmerman interjected. "But what if they change their mind?"

"If that happens, come back. Don't push your luck. Do you understand what I'm saying?" Esposito said.

All the men shook their heads.

"Anyone else have a question?" All remained quiet. "All right then, let's do it!"

Wearing jungle fatigues with their faces smeared in green and black grease paint, all five commandoes left the barracks. Outside, they separated into groups of two.

Zimmerman and Viera were the first to reach their destination. The previous afternoon was washday, and the mama-sans had hung wet clothes out to dry. The possessions were the personal belongings of nurses from the New Zealand Surgical Team who worked on the same compound. For the commandoes the pickings appeared incredibly easy. With the flashlight pointing toward the clothesline, Zimmerman said to Viera, "Go get 'em, buddy." Viera, as if in a frenzy, had a virtual field day ripping off the clothespins while stuffing the bras and panties down his shirt. He seemed to be having too much fun. Zimmerman finally had to intercede. "That's enough. Let's get out of here before someone wakes up."

"That's a Roger," said Viera as each turned around and started their dash but not before running smack-dab into a stealth clothesline.

The men hit the ground as if struck by a bullet. Viera dropped the underwear on the ground. The commotion was enough to wake several of the nurses. Lights from the barracks began to appear from the screened window openings, and both men realized it was time to hightail it out of there. Viera picked up what he could see in the semi-darkness. Zimmerman did the same. In a flash, they ran back toward the operations center.

Pasquale wasn't as fortunate. When he arrived, nothing was left hanging on the clothesline, not even a pair of socks. Earlier in the day the mama-sans had taken everything down. *Just great*, he thought. *Now what'll I do?* He had little time to think or react. Just then he was startled by a loud noise emanating from the adjacent area. It was Zimmerman and Viera crashing into the clothesline. At the time, he hadn't a clue what was happening or who had caused the ruckus. The Donut Dollies were now turning on the lights in the Red Cross barracks nearly as fast as a machine gun fires rounds. Upholding his reputation not to be shut out, Pasquale decided to take the matter into his own hands. Within close proximity of an open window he yelled, "This is a panty raid. Throw out your underwear."

"Who are you?" a feminine voice inquired from a window.

"A horny GI," Pasquale responded. "Now throw out your underwear or I'll come in and get it myself."

No sooner did the words leave his lips than several screens opened and a few scantily clad women threw out several of their precious and personal possessions. Quickly the corporal picked them up and stuffed them down his shirt. Looking at one of the nurses hanging out of the window, he said before departing, "Have a nice night, ma'am!"

Pasquale made his departure just seconds before MP's arrived on the scene. Apparently a Red Cross volunteer didn't take kindly to the intrusion and telephoned security. The call came a bit late. Pasquale was not apprehended.

Meanwhile, Zalinski and Canty had no problem maneuvering past the guards, as Zalinski was a friend of one of them. Crossing the road was like a walk in the park with no traffic or pedestrians.

Zalinski grabbed Canty and said, "Let's walk between the hooches. This afternoon I saw socks and underwear hanging on a clothesline."

"Okay," Canty responded.

After walking in the dark through a maze of alleyways for twenty minutes, the men became disoriented. Not long after, a dog got a whiff of their scent and started barking. Zalinski panicked. Looking at Canty he exclaimed, "Let's get the hell out here!" as he hastily bolted from the scene. Little did he realize, Canty never followed. The private had his own agenda and was determined to succeed, something he had difficulty accomplishing most of his life. For several minutes, he leaned against a wall of a hooch until the dog quieted down. Sensing that the coast was clear, he forged ahead. As he passed each hooch, Canty shined his flashlight in the open window. After several minutes of searching, he came upon a teenage damsel sound asleep in her bed. *This looks interesting*, he thought. Cautiously, he walked to the front door and, to his surprise, discovered it wasn't locked. Gently, he pushed the door open. Using the flashlight, he made his way to the young mama-san's bedroom. Seeing her, he walked toward the bed all the while looking for a bureau, which, he surmised, would hold the treasure he was so gallantly seeking. But as he did, he accidentally knocked over a small, clay flowerpot. The noise was hardly audible, but it was enough to wake up the poor maiden who was now in utter distress. Canty thought fast. In a panic, he jumped off his feet and lunged toward the bed. The mama-san tried to react, but Canty was able to cover her mouth with one of his large hands just in time to muffle her cry. No one heard her plea. Pulling out his handkerchief, he stuffed it in her mouth. Although preventing her from screaming, she wouldn't stop squirming. Thinking fast, he pulled off the pillowcase and tied her hands behind her back. Now only her feet were kicking. Canty pulled off the sheet and wrapped it around her legs. Finally she was restrained. As if by divine intervention, he got a bright idea: *Why rifle through the bureau to get her underwear when I can bring back the real thing?* The young mama-san was already half-naked with her breasts fully exposed. All she was wearing was a pair of white panties. Hoping there wouldn't be a commotion, he slung her over his shoulders and walked out the door. Not long after, he reached the relative safety of the compound. The security guards were baffled. GI's had run across the street many times to knock-off a piece of ass, but nobody had ever brought one back.

Esposito repeated the question. "Have any of you guys got any bright ideas; come on, anything?"

After a while, Pasquale answered. "Yeah, I think I do, Sarge."

"And what's that?"

"Why don't we just bring her back?"

"Say again!"

"Why don't we go over there and just bring her back?" repeated Pasquale.

"Do you honestly think you can waltz right over to her hooch, release her to her family, and say, 'we're sorry we kidnapped you daughter, but now we want to give her back.' Shit, man. Are you crazy? Forget it. Besides, you can't even speak the language. Come on; get real, huh!"

"Listen to me, Sarge! I can speak enough Vietnamese to get by. I know a little French, too, and being Italian, I can communicate with my hands. Between the three, I'll be okay. Come on, Sarge. It's the only way. A few of us will go back to the village, give her back to her family, apologize, and then leave."

"It'll never work."

"Well, there is something else we can do."

"And what's that?"

Pasquale gazed at Esposito for a second or two, then the others. "We'll give the papa-san a peace offering, you know, a payoff. It's the only way we'll be able to smooth things over."

"You think he'll accept it and keep his mouth shut?"

"Did you ever know a papa-san who couldn't be bought?"

"Well . . . no, but this is some pretty serious shit."

"Trust me Sarge. I did this kind of stuff all the time back home."

"Well . . . what'll you need?"

"I'd say two or three cartons of cigarettes, Salem if possible, a case of Coke and 40 to 50 dollars in MPC's. With that we should be able to return his daughter without fear and maybe help him pay off the mortgage on his friggin' hooch," as he laughed.

Esposito grinned. "You know, I think it just might work. Who's gonna go with you?"

"I'll take him," pointing at Viera, "and him," as he motioned toward Canty.

"No, not him!" Esposito exclaimed. "He's the idiot that got us into this mess in the first place. Why do you need him?"

"Because he's the only guy in the company strong enough to carry her back to the village."

Esposito knew Pasquale was right, although he had a hard time admitting it. "All right, damn it! Let's get this over with!" After Esposito approved the operation, three of them, along with the captive slung over Canty's right shoulder, departed. The time was 0120.

Forty-five minutes elapsed before the men returned. It had been an eternity for Esposito.

Esposito was anxious. "How'd you make out?" he said as the men straggled in from the compound.

"Hell. It was easier than I thought!" Pasquale exclaimed, still trying to catch his breath after running part way across the compound.

"Well?"

"Sarge, you wouldn't believe it!"

"Why wouldn't I?"

"Because the papa-san never even knew his daughter was missing. We had to wake the son-of-a-bitch."

"No shit?"

"No shit! I had to shake him several times before he woke up."

Suddenly, Canty barged through the door; huffing and puffing like a hound dog on a hot summer day.

Pasquale continued without acknowledging the intrusion. "After the gook came to his senses, we explained everything to him and apologized for our stupid mistake." Pasquale was using his hands and arms to express himself just as he always did during a

33

conversation. "He was more scared seeing us at that hour than angry about the particulars. I told Viera and Canty to place all the stuff on the floor next to his bed at the same time telling the papa-san that this was our way of saying we were sorry." Pasquale snickered. "As long as I live, I'll never forget the expression on his face. He was the happiest gook I've ever seen — I mean, the guy thought he died and went to heaven. Sarge let me tell you. He was so damn excited about his new found wealth, he completely forgot about what happened to his daughter."

Esposito burst out laughing. For the first time that night, he finally felt relieved. "But will he keep quiet?" he asked apprehensively.

"You can bet your ass on it!"

"How can you be sure?"

"Because . . . after we gave him all the stuff, I looked him straight in the eye and said, 'If you tell a single soul about what happened tonight, I'm gonna come back and wring your friggin' neck.'"

Like precision clockwork, at exactly 6 a.m., the morning bugler played his wake-up call. A half-hour later, the battalion began falling out for morning formation. As the soldiers strolled from their barracks, they couldn't help but notice a strange display at the northern end of the compound. First there were a few chuckles. Eventually, as more soldiers became aware, the snickers turned into a loud crescendo of laughter that echoed throughout the quadrangle. The laughter continued unabated for a few minutes until the colonel arrived in his Jeep.

Stepping out of the vehicle with his aide following close behind, the colonel walked toward the flagpole. Looking up, he noticed something unexpected. Turning toward his aide he said, "I see that the natives were restless last night."

Hours earlier, Esposito had been busy. He had been stringing woman's underwear to the rope of the battalion flagpole until the garments ran two-thirds its length.

The lieutenant appeared more puzzled and embarrassed by the display of feminine attire than the colonel.

"Lieutenant," said the colonel.

"What, Sir?"

"Have your men take the clothes down so that we can go ahead with raising the Colors."

"Yes, Sir!" said the lieutenant. Turning toward the flag detail, he gave the soldiers a stern order. "Men. Take those things down immediately!" Muffled chatter and restrained laughter could still be heard in the background.

As the bras and panties were hastily lowered, the colonel leaned toward the lieutenant and whispered in his ear, "I wonder who filled those cups?" The lieutenant gave a half-smile not sure how to react to the colonel's uncharacteristic behavior.

Order was quickly restored and in less time than it takes to fleece a drunken bum, the underwear was removed and placed in the back of the Jeep, presumably for eventual disposal. From that moment on, the morning flag raising ceremony proceeded without incident.

The raid had succeeded beyond Esposito's wildest imagination.

Esposito had achieved his primary goal . . . er, no, it wasn't about making GI's horny or embarrassing the brass by flying the Colors (red, white, blue, green, and yellow bras and panties on the battalion flagpole), though it could be argued that that's what was intended. On the contrary, the purpose was something far more important and longer lasting. On the morning of February 17, 1969, at battalion headquarters in Qui Nhon, Vietnam, Esposito's ad-hoc team of commando support personnel had managed to rekindle the flickering flame of a smoldering campfire. It was every soldier's burning desire and, undoubtedly, the most important weapon employed against boredom while serving in a rear echelon unit. Yes! On that day, morale was finally restored to a group of young men in a battalion very much in need.

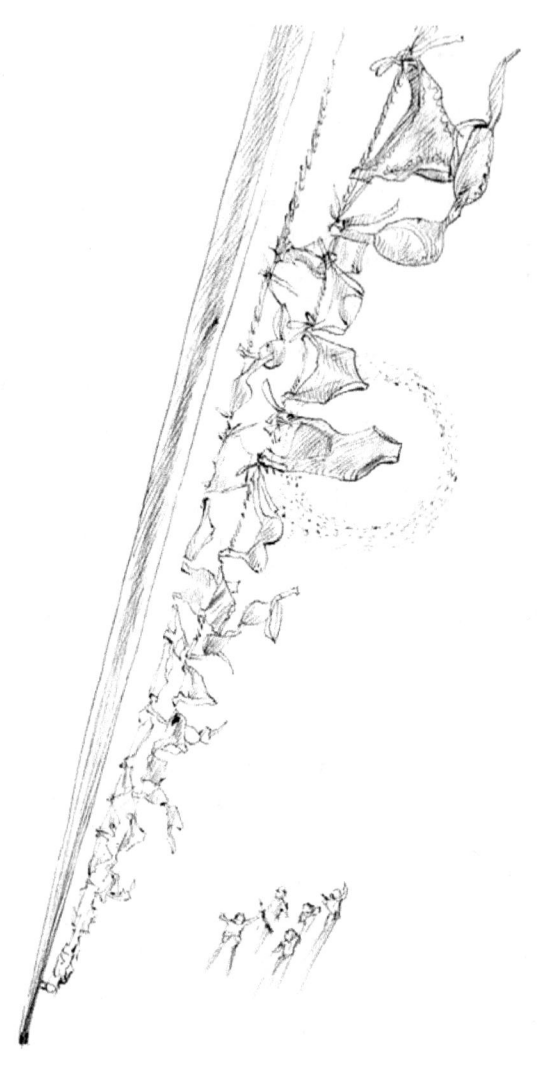

The Spoils of War

DINNER IS SERVED

Bring hither the fatted calf and kill it; and let us eat, and be merry.
-Bible, *Luke* 15:23

Hông was twenty. She appeared much older. Unmarried, she lived with her parents and twelve year-old sister less than a mile from our compound. Hông also had two brothers, both ARVN soldiers serving in an artillery unit somewhere near Da Nang.

No one knew if Hông made it through grade school before her family sent her out to toil in the rice paddies. She never discussed it. From dawn to dusk, she faced an unmerciful and relentless sun. Conceivably, that is what aged her. After five seasons of planting and harvesting rice, Hông found an occupation more to her liking. The work was easier and the pay incomparable, at least by Vietnamese standards. She was hired as a mama-san for American GI's at a headquarters company.

Since the day Rudy and Marcus first arrived in 'Nam, Hông washed their laundry, ironed their clothes, dusted, and cleaned their barracks. They were not the only beneficiaries of her domestic services as she performed similar duties for all the others assigned to the motor pool. Hông was a surrogate mother, but unlike everyone else's mother, she was paid to do housework. The wage was slave labor reasonable — $2.00 a man per week or $20.00 for all ten of us. Nobody ever complained about the quality of her work or the cost. Hông, too, was satisfied. Earning over a $1,000 a year was a sizable sum considering the annual per capita income of South Vietnam was less than $125.

Hông never had to concern herself about equipment or supplies. GI's purchased the iron and ironing board years ago. When powdered detergent, bleach or spray starch needed replenishing, the men pitched in their fair share, usually no more than a few dollars a month. Someone would run to the PX and buy

37

the items; and, bingo, she was back in business. Rudy, the motor pool sergeant, collected the fees on payday (the last day of every month) and gave Hông her wages usually in MPC's (military payment certificates).

"Hey, guys! Tomorrow's Hông's birthday. What say we kick in a few extra bucks and give her something for her birthday?" asked Rudy.

"What'll we get her for a gift?" Marcus asked.

"I think she would appreciate money. With it, she can double the value and buy what she wants on the black market."

"Let's do it then," Marcus said. No one felt the need for further discussion.

Hông was well liked so collecting the money was easy. Within minutes, Rudy had 40 MPC's with the purple-colored engraving of a fighter pilot on the back of each bill. "This'll do just fine," he said. "When she comes by tomorrow to pick up our dirty laundry, I'll give her the cash."

The following morning, Rudy and Marcus waited patiently for Hông's arrival. Sitting on separate bunks, they listened intently to the latest Dylan album. When Hông came into the room, she was startled to see the men. Immediately, Rudy pushed himself up off the bunk and approached her. "On behalf of all the guys," he said, "we'd like to wish you a Happy Birthday," while handing her the envelope.

As was her meek and mild manner, she looked down at her feet. Extending her hand she accepted the envelope and said, "Thank you for your kindness." Hông had no difficulty with the English language.

More than a week passed before Rudy and Marcus ran into Hông at the barracks near the bottom of the stairs. As usual, she was squatting, washing clothes. After noticing the men, she stood and approached them. Bowing her head almost to her waist, she said softly, "My family would be honored if both of you could dine with us this Sunday." Rudy and Marcus were caught off guard,

38

though each should have known better. Asians were that way. When you give a gift to an Asian, expect something in return. The trait was deeply imbedded in their culture. Hông couldn't invite the entire motor pool but if she could, she would. Rudy and Marcus were the most likely choices.

"Yes, I'll come," Rudy said. Then he looked at Marcus and asked, "What about you?"

"Why sure," Marcus replied. "I can use some good home cookin' right about now."

Sunday at noon, Rudy and Marcus borrowed a Jeep from the motor pool and drove to Hông's home. The ride took only a few minutes. Hông met both men at the front door. Dressed in her finest garments, a dark purple *ao dais* — a high-collar, long silk gown slit to the thigh — she was a sight to behold. Underneath, she wore black silk pants. She looked every bit the hostess. "Please come in," she said, in perfect English. Hông may not have had a formal education, but her time spent working for the Americans made her English almost flawless. As was the custom, both men took off their shoes before entering.

"I would like to introduce you to my family," Hông said bashfully. "This is my father." He was a short man even by Vietnamese standards, barely reaching five-feet two. If ever there stood a candidate for elevated sandals, Hong's father would have been the first to qualify. The papa-san bowed and smiled, but said nothing. Rudy and Marcus, not knowing what to do, did the same. "This is my mother." She, too, bowed, and so did we. She also remained speechless. "And this is my sister, Tuyêt."

Tuyêt spoke only one word in Vietnamese that even Rudy and Marcus understood. "*Chào.*"

The men returned the greeting. "*Chào.*"

Mama-San and Daughter Tuyệt

"My parents do not understand your language, so please be patient," Hông advised.

Rudy felt the need to calm her fears. "Hông. I speak reasonably good Vietnamese, so everything will be just fine. Before I forget, please tell your sister that I like her name. It's an unusual name for this part of the world. It means snow, doesn't it?"

"Yes, it does," she responded. "You understand Vietnamese quite well."

"Thank you," Rudy said. "The army sent me to school to learn your language."

Hông turned to speak to her sister. Tuyêt blushed as she listened. She told Hông something in Vietnamese, but Rudy failed to catch the words.

Hông translated. "Tuyêt appreciated your comment and thanks you. She said you are a handsome soldier."

"Please tell her, 'thank you.'"

Hong complied. "*Cám ón ông.*"

Hiding her face with her arm, Tuyêt giggled.

The smell of the open pit fire and the delectable aroma of barbecued meat made both men salivate. Months of eating C-rations and mess food prepared them well for the dining extravaganza. Marcus looked at Rudy and said, "Take a whiff of that."

"I know," he said. "Smells good, huh?"

With a slow but deliberate swoop of his arm, papa-san directed us toward the dining area. Hông showed Rudy and Marcus where to kneel. Each man was assigned a select place at the table. Rudy and Marcus took their places next to each other while papa-san and mama-san sat directly across from them. Hông and Tuyêt sat at opposite ends of the table.

Before long, mama-san pushed herself away from the table and stood. With a labored bow, and speaking in Vietnamese, she obviously excused herself. Marcus had not a clue what she said or intended to do. For Marcus, the Vietnamese language was a huge problem, so he held his tongue. Within minutes, mama-san was back cradling a large, wooden bowl of soup. The broth was the

41

weakest mixture Marcus had ever laid eyes on, nearly colorless as water. It wasn't Campbell's Soup, Marcus thought, that's for sure. Things that looked like tiny green vegetables swirled around on top. Mama-san poured the soup in separate cups and handed them to each of us. Papa-san lifted his cup and took the first sip. Looking at his wife, papa-san's eyes expressed satisfaction if not sheer delight. Hông and Tuyêt picked up their cups and followed suit. Following their lead, Rudy and Marcus did the same. After tasting the mixture, Rudy said to himself, *The soup is hot; other than that, it's tasteless.*

After finishing the soup, mama-san and Hông picked up the empty cups and excused themselves. A short time later, they reentered the room carrying small bowls of salad. Much to Rudy's satisfaction, the greens were recognizable. There were bean sprouts, spinach and lettuce. All were finely diced with no piece larger than a half-inch in circumference. Marcus looked around the table for salad dressing but saw none. Not one to complain, he said nothing. There was, however, a small plate on the table filled with a substance resembling a brownish-black sauce. Marcus leaned toward Rudy and asked, "What's that?"

Whispering in Marcus's ear, Rudy said, "I don't think you want to try that."

"Why not?"

"Because it's *nuoc-mum*, fish sauce to you, brother."

Rudy's candor couldn't have come at a better time. Marcus gave him one of those looks like *thanks for the warning* being coy so Hông and her family wouldn't see his bitter expression.

Papa-san took the first taste but not before drowning his salad with the sauce. He liked it. Seeing papa-san happy, Rudy decided to take a bite while skipping the enhancer. He looked at his friend and said, "Not bad," which to Marcus meant, eat it, it won't kill you.

After finishing the second course, Rudy initiated a discussion with papa-san. Marcus hadn't a clue about their conversation as it was all gibberish to him. Marcus continued to kneel with a perpetual smile on his face, feeling about as awkward as a Boy

Scout who accidentally stumbled upon a nudist colony in the woods.

Several minutes elapsed before papa-san excused himself. The main course was about to arrive. Neither man could wait. The aroma of the roast was making them crazy with hunger. Speaking English, Rudy, Hông and Marcus engaged in small talk.

A quarter of an hour elapsed before papa-san reentered the room. In his hands he carried a huge platter. Marcus thought he recognized the smell: roast lamb. *I haven't had lamb since Ma made it. How'd they manage to get lamb in 'Nam? Maybe it's imported from New Zealand. Ahhh, who cares? It smells great*, he thought.

The presentation was exquisite. The head had been removed prior to cooking. The legs were severed at the body and placed along side. The entire chest cavity had been gutted. Surrounding the lamb were colorful vegetables and exotic tropical fruits. The juices were still bubbling on the serving tray. To Marcus, it seemed a cardinal sin to violate the design.

Before any of them began to eat, papa-san said a prayer. Upon completion, he turned toward the men, gestured with his hand, which to them signified it was time to dig in. Marcus didn't need an interpreter to figure out the message. He grabbed a hindquarter and placed it on his plate. Nobody had utensils, so Marcus waited to see papa-san's next move. Papa-san selected a leg. Wiping his hand with his napkin to remove the grease, he picked up the leg and took a bite from the fattest portion. Papa-san groaned in ecstasy. That's all Marcus needed. Using his hands, he brought the leg to his mouth and took an enormous bite. Slowly, he chewed while savoring the taste. Then, he swallowed. *This is delicious*, he thought, not like Ma's back home, but still kinda tasty.

After taking a second bite, chewing and swallowing again, he looked over at Rudy and said, "Tell papa-san that the lamb is delicious."

"Okay," Rudy said. After getting the papa-san's attention, Marcus heard Rudy say, "*Ngon cùu.*"

"*Cùu?*" the papa-san said with a surprised expression.

"*Cùu câm?*" Rudy asked again. "*Món kia la gi?*"

The papa-san said something in return. All Marcus caught was "*con chó.*"

Rudy stopped short before taking a bite. "What's wrong, man? The lamb is superb," Marcus said.

"Look at the leg on your plate."

"Okay."

"Take a good look," Rudy said as he pointed to the blackened meat on Marcus's plate.

Marcus was eating a leg all right, but there wasn't a hoof. The bottom portion, although charred from the roasting, had a few pads remaining from a . . . gulp . . . paw.

"Damn!" he said. Looking at Hông, Marcus asked, "What are we eating?"

Hông responded, "We're having one of my people's favorite delicacies, *con chó!*"

"What's *con chó*? Marcus asked.

"Dog."

"Dog!" Marcus said, not wanting to believe what he had heard.

"Yes, dog. Dogs are scarce and in such high demand; my father was lucky to have found one to please you."

Now green, and not with envy, Marcus looked toward Rudy and away from Hông so she wouldn't hear him. "'Lucky,' she says." Then it dawned on him. "Rudy, when was the last time you saw the dog Lucky?"

"Why? Oh . . . "

"For God's sake, man! We're eating dog . . . maybe Lucky!' We're like . . . well . . . like cannibals."

"No," said Rudy correcting him. "You're eating dog. Remember . . . , I didn't take a bite."

Turning back toward Hông, Marcus said, "Excuse me. I have to go outside for a minute."

"Is everything all right?" Hông asked.

"Yes, yes. Just let me get a breath of fresh air. I'll be right back."

After leaving his lunch behind the hooch, Marcus gathered his composure long enough to walk back inside. The platter of dog had been removed.

"Are you sure you are all right?" Hông asked again.

"Thanks. Yes, I'm much better. Must have been something I ate . . ." then he caught himself . . . "last night."

Rudy smirked.

As far as Marcus was concerned, dinner was over.

Before departing Rudy thanked the entire family. Speaking to the mama-san, he said, "*Bà cho ä ngon quá.*"

Marcus said good-bye in English.

During the ride back in the Jeep, Marcus asked Rudy what he said to the mama-san as he was leaving the hooch.

"I told her that the meal was delicious."

"What?" Marcus said.

"I was just trying to be polite."

"I guess I can understand. But what I'd really like to know is how you avoided eating any of the meat."

"I took a leg on my plate," Rudy said, obviously proud to reveal his technique. "I made a few cuts and pushed the meat aside. When no one was looking, I scooped it up in my hand and put it in my pocket. From time to time, I'd motion toward my mouth and make believe I was taking a bite. Then I'd start chewing and fake a swallow. You know...they never caught on."

Suddenly, Marcus noticed Rudy was speeding. "Hey, Rudy!" he said. "Why the rush?"

"I can't wait to get the damned dog meat out of my pocket and change into clean fatigues!

A LITTLE TAIL

What men call gallantry, and gods adultery,
is more common where the climate's sultry.
-Lord Byron, *Don Juan* (1819-1824)

"Hey, numbnuts! When was the last time ya got laid?"

The question seemed to materialize out of nowhere. Though Neilan's tone of voice sounded disdainful and the message vulgar, it was far from unacceptable behavior in a country were ill manners and four-letter words were as commonplace as overhead projectiles and exploding mortars.

"You talking to me?" Rodrigues asked.

"Yeah, you! Who the hell do you think I'm talkin' to?" replied Neilan.

Glancing back, Rodrigues sighed as he rubbed his face with the long end of a tattered towel draped around his neck. While mulling a response, he unfastened a canteen from his web belt, opened the twist-off spout, and proceeded to remove his helmet. Lifting the canteen above his head he poured what amounted to a full cup of water over his dirty and greasy hair. *Oh baby this feels good*, he thought. As the warm, iodized water trickled down his forehead and cheeks, it intermingled with body fluids that reeked of salt. Immediately his eyes began to sting and his vision blurred. Using the same damp, olive green towel, he briskly wiped his eyes. Slowly his vision returned. Before re-attaching the canteen, he took a few quick swigs to quench his insatiable thirst, making sure not to spill what little remained of the precious liquid.

"Well?" asked Neilan. "Are you holding out on me, man?"

Rodrigues tried to deflect the question.

"You know . . . it's been so damn long I can't remember."

The reply was fabricated, but he knew of no other way to prevent the superfluous inquiry. Today, he was walking point, a position in the platoon he never relished. The responsibility was enormous. He knew it. Performing double-duty, he looked for trip wires while peering ahead and above for movement in the underbrush and trees. He also listened for noises: Vietnamese chattering in their native tongue not knowing whether friend or foe, the slashing of jungle underbrush by an unconfirmed scout, and yes, even squawking birds. Silence was an unwelcome companion because it usually meant trouble.

Neilan had been in country for several months. Although it wasn't the right time to engage in political debate or conduct philosophical discussions, he knew that taking about sex relieved the tension, even in the bush.

Today, the platoon was operating in a secure area. Base camp was less than twenty clicks away. Over the past week a bulldozer crew from an engineering battalion had cleared the area of most trees and nearly all the vegetation that could have concealed the enemy. Although no walk in the park, the danger level was low.

"You're always getting brain farts, you know that, Rodrigues, don't you?" Neilan jokingly responded as he shifted his M16A1 rifle from one shoulder to the other. The weapon only weighed 8.2 pounds, but after humping the bush for several hours, it seemed like twenty. "Now come on, man, think hard. When was the last time you got a piece of ass?" If Neilan was anything, he was persistent.

Rodrigues hesitated. God, this guy's never going to let up. "Give me a minute," he said.

Moving forward at a snail's pace and listening to Neilan for nearly a half-hour, Rodrigues decided, "Enough is enough." He knew better. The inquisition would continue until Neilan got what he wanted. "All right, Neilan, for Christ's sake! If I tell you, will you get off my ass?"

"You know it, man!"

Neilan quickly closed the gap in the line, as he listened to Rodrigues coerced confession.

"It happened a few weeks ago back at the fire base. It was the night you and Dwyer were playing cribbage, listening to the Stones, and smoking joints. Remember?"

"No . . . not really. That kind of shit we do all the time."

Rodrigues appeared a bit frustrated as he continued.

"You know. The night you and Dwyer almost got in a fistfight when he accused you of cheating while pegging your score."

"Oh yeah! That night! I was wondering where the hell you were. So tell us what happened. We want to hear all the dirty little details. Right, guys?"

"Well, I guess I was feeling kinda' horny that night and..."

"Shit, man! You're always horny," Neilan interjected. "You know, Rodrigues? Did you ever wonder why I don't take a shower standing next to you? I'm afraid if I ever dropped the soap you'd be all over me."

Those within earshot laughed hysterically.

Corporal Sullivan, carrying an M-60 machine-gun, added his own two-cents.

"I always wondered about you, Rodrigues. Now, there's no disputing it!" Everyone laughed but no one more than Dwyer; a tall, gangly kid reigning out of the Philadelphia suburbs. His laugh was odd and annoying, not unlike an African hyena.

"And what are you laughing at, Dwyer?" Neilan interjected. "It's about time you realize that sex isn't always performed solo."

"Up yours!"

"Wow! Now there's an earthshaking remark — 'Up yours'." Neilan said.

Dwyer could take a joke like the next guy, but he didn't appreciate the comment and how it was delivered. "And I suppose you think you're a incredible stud?" Dwyer shot back.

"I don't think . . . I know! Face it, Dwyer. You're sexually challenged."

The conversation was starting to get heated, and Lieutenant Murphy finally had to intercede. "Quiet down!" he ordered. Though he couldn't admit it to his men, he, too, was enjoying the banter.

After waiting a few minutes to appease the lieutenant, Neilan broke the silence. "Well, are you going to tell us the story?"

"Only if you guys promise to shut the hell up!"

"You won't hear another word from any of us. Right, guys?"

"That's a fact, Jack!" said Sullivan. The others mumbled in agreement.

"Oh, one other thing. Lieutenant?"

"What, Corporal?"

"Promise you won't use what I say against me; not that it's bad or anything?"

"Corporal. What's said out here stays out here. Just keep your voice down."

The men were fortunate. Lieutenant Murphy was cool. He was a regular guy who just happened to be an officer, unlike their previous lieutenant who DEROS'd back to the World four months earlier.

"Thanks, Lieutenant. Okay, listen up 'cause I'm only going to tell it once! I guess I was just overcome by the urge and besides; you and Dwyer were stoned so I decided to take a little vacation for myself. I walked through the compound and out the main gate."

"You didn't get stopped by the security guards?" Neilan asked, looking a bit surprised.

"I thought you said you wouldn't interrupt?" Rodrigues shot back.

"I couldn't help it. After all, the village is off-limits. Ya should have been challenged."

"Hell no! Why should they? They knew I wasn't going AWOL. Besides, I knew them. They let me cross into the village all the time." Now smiling, Rodrigues turned toward Neilan and said, "Ya know, it doesn't hurt to bribe the guards once and a while with a couple cartons of cigarettes."

"So that's how you did it!" Neilan responded with astonishment.

Just then a call came in over the radio. The lieutenant took the phone from the RTO, listened for a second, and then relayed their present coordinates. Within twenty minutes a chopper would be coming in to pick them up and bring them back to the compound.

Lieutenant Murphy ordered the squad to halt. "We'll wait here for pickup," he said.

The men gathered together and sat down near the shade of a small tree, one that hadn't been leveled by the work of the engineering battalion.

But before their departure, Neilan wanted to hear more about Rodrigues' escapades. Speaking to the back of Rodrigues' head, he said, "All right, let's hear the rest."

Rodrigues spun around and faced Neilan. "Look!" he replied. "It was one of those slam, bam, thank you ma'am things. It was nothin' special."

"Bullshit!" said Neilan. "Ya gotta tell us the entire story!"

"There's not much to tell," Rodrigues said as he again wiped the sweat from his eyes with his towel. "I got to the whorehouse in less than two minutes by running through the small alleys and between the hooches. I knocked on the back door and an elderly mama-san answered. If I remember right, she had dollar signs written in her eyes." Neilan chuckled along with the others. "She immediately invited me in. That's when the negotiations started. I offered $10 MPC; she wanted $20 MPC. We finally agreed on $10 MPC and two packs of cigarettes."

Sullivan jumped back into the conversation. "Hey, good deal, man!"

Rodrigues acknowledged the remark by slightly lifting and nodding his hand as if to say thanks.

The patrol soon came to a halt. Rodrigues couldn't wait to talk about his meandering ways only to get Neilan off his case. He continued: "She took me to a side room where I found myself staring by six or seven half-naked females. Before I knew it, I was surrounded. One said to me, 'Me numba one virgin!' Another started groping me all over while saying things like 'Me give GI boom-boom!' and 'Me make GI very happy!' Then the others came over and every single one told me that they were virgins. I mean I almost died. It was funny, man! I said to myself, Vietnam must have more virgins than any other country on the face of this planet." Neilan and the others couldn't help but laugh again.

Lieutenant Murphy had to speak up a second time. "All right, men, hold it down."

After a few seconds of silence, Rodrigues continued. "Ya know . . . ya have to wonder. With all the self-proclaimed virgins in this country, why are there so many people? Not waiting for an answer, he said, "It must have been the influx of women refugees from Thailand, China, Laos, and Cambodia." The men laughed but in a more subdued tone. Nobody wanted to upset the lieutenant.

Rodrigues continued. "One gal looked kinda nice — ya know as far as gooks go — so I chose her. The madam escorted us to a side room and left us alone. Slowly she undressed me. Before long I was all over her, pulling her clothes off and throwing them on the concrete floor. Hell! As far as tricks go, Houdini could have learned a few." He paused then said, "It didn't take me long after that. Without a doubt, it must have been the fastest buck she ever earned." All the members of the platoon were now zoned into the conversation.

Rodrigues mulled over whether to tell them the entire story. *Should I? Ah, what the hell. I might as well. If they haven't heard it yet, they probably will as soon as we return to base camp*, he thought.

"After we finished having sex, I lit a cigarette and just laid on the bed. It wasn't that I was comfortable or that I even liked her. I just wanted to relax and not think about the military shit any more. Ya' know what I mean, man?" Most of the platoon nodded in acceptance.

"She was lying next to me, butt-ass naked. All I had on was my green boxers and my unlaced combat boots. There I was, minding my own damned business when suddenly, I heard a ruckus. Someone was banging on the front door. I figured it was another horny GI like me."

Rodrigues paused for a moment to light a cigarette. As he breathed in the smoke, he held it in his lungs before releasing it with one long exhale. Looking at Neilan first and then the others, he continued to tell his tale.

"All of a sudden the commotion was making its way toward my room. I remember hearing loud voices speaking in Vietnamese and you didn't have to understand the language to know it wasn't a

51

pleasant conversation or, for that matter, a welcoming committee." All the while, Rodrigues became more animated, swaying his hands back and forth, up and down. "Suddenly, I'm staring eye-to-eye with an irate papa-san standing in the doorway. As fate would have it, he's pointing this huge machete at my chest."

"Holy shit!" said Neilan.

"I mean there wasn't any time to think," Rodrigues continued. "I had to act. Looking back, I suspect the gal I laid was his daughter, and he didn't take kindly to her new profession or me as her client."

"Leaving the rest of my clothes, I leaped headfirst out the window. Unable to break my fall, my jaw hit the ground. There I was, lying waist deep in a shallow cesspool. As fast as I could, I dragged myself out, picked myself up, and ran through the alleys, across the street and back to the safety of our compound. Whether the old bastard chased me or not, I don't know 'cause I never looked back."

About this time, Neilan was laughing hysterically and hardly able to speak. So were the others. Gaining what little composure he could muster, Neilan asked Rodrigues a final question.

"What did the guards do when they saw you in that condition?"

"They laughed their asses off, just like you sorry bastards are doing." Then it dawned on him as he said, "I apologize! I didn't mean you, Lieutenant!"

"I know," responded the Lieutenant.

The sound of a low-flying chopper could be heard coming in over the horizon. Lieutenant Murphy was the first to stand.

"Okay men; the show's over. Move it out!" he ordered, as he pointed toward a clearing where the chopper was about to land.

Neilan reiterated, "You heard the Lieutenant. Move it out!" as he, too, pushed himself up off the ground. But before he could get to his feet, Rodrigues interrupted.

"Sarge?"

"What?" Neilan asked.

"When's the last time you got laid?"

Papa-San Wields a Mean Machete

"None of your damn business. But remember somethin'."

"And what's that?" Rodrigues asked.

"With rank come privileges. That's all you need to know," Neilan said with a devilish grin. "Now get your sorry asses on the chopper, and let's get the hell out of here."

THE REVELATION
ACCORDING TO CABRAL

I have a rendezvous with Death
At some disputed barricade.
-Alan Seegar, *I Have a Rendezvous with Death*

O nly vague images could be seen through the thick, silver-gray fog, a fog that enveloped the entire staging area. In spite of the poor visibility, an occasional break in the haze revealed a paucity of soldiers, perhaps 20 in all, each dressed in combat fatigues. Several held small arms weapons. Those without rifles tucked their hands beneath their armpits trying to stave off the early morning chill, a Vietnamese chill not to be confused with the crisp late October weather of New England, where temperatures could plummet from the high-sixties to the low-thirties in less than an hour. It was seventy-eight degrees, but to those who had become accustomed to the scorching sun and mid-afternoon temperatures hovering between 100 and 110, it felt downright frigid.

For infantry soldiers serving in this God-forsaken land, it was an accepted norm — although a highly undesirable one — to be wakened early in the morning and ordered into another hot LZ. On this day, however, something seemed strikingly peculiar. The abrupt wake-up and the fast-spreading fog may have triggered the uneasiness. Perhaps it was nothing more than a gut feeling, the kind of queasiness infantrymen experience before a combat mission. But maybe, just maybe, it was something worse. No matter the explanation, each of them had reached their emotional threshold, frightened far beyond any fear they ever imagined.

Near the staging area stood Sergeant David Nolan, a draftee, who only a few months previous had been promoted to his present rank. At 22, Nolan was the oldest member of his squad.

Nolan loved to joke and nothing gave him greater pleasure than to badger his men about his newly acquired status. Nearing the end of his tour, he would crow like a rooster, "You know why I'm better than you? I'm better than you because, I'm a 'short-timer!'" With less than 40 days to serve in-country, Nolan held, what he thought was, the trump card. His entire tenure had been served while fighting as a foot soldier in the steamy jungles and muddy rice paddies of South Vietnam. He figured: In less than two months, I'll be back home chasing skirts and putting this stupid war behind me.

Fatigued and upset, compounded more so by an annoying mosquito buzzing relentlessly around his head, Nolan broke the silence. "Murph," he said. "Listen to me, man! Yesterday we got our asses kicked, yet here we are again getting ready to head out to the bush. Who the hell do they think we are?"

The longer he pontificated, the more deliberate, incendiary, and venomous his voice became. "Ya know what bothers me, Murph?"

"What's that?" Murphy asked.

"Nobody gives a damn," Nolan replied, as he continued to swat at the pesky mosquito that was starting to get on his nerves. "We're just numbers. That's all . . . nothin' but friggin' numbers. I'll tell ya, man. If I'm wasted today, it'd be a blessing, 'cause I can't take it anymore." Pausing but a moment, he looked at Murphy, hardly able to contain his feeling of disgust as he vented the last of his frustration. "I've got nothin' left, ya hear me, Murph? Nothin'. I'm fuckin' beat; as drained as a keg of beer after an all night frat party."

"I know how you feel, man," Murphy replied. "I'm in full agreement."

Although spent physically and emotionally, Nolan's reflexes remained keen. With lightning speed, he slapped the mosquito against his forehead. The attack proved lethal, leaving bits of smeared insect on the right side of his forehead but, strangely, no red smidgen of blood that usually accompanies such a bite. "Gotcha, ya little bastard!" he extolled with an exuberance that bordered on macabre delight.

56

Specialist Five Brian Murphy, a redheaded Irish kid looking more like a high school valedictorian (which he was) than a combat infantryman, astutely grasped the reason for Nolan's tirade. Cocking his head back and gazing directly at his friend, he said, "Dave, obviously the bastards think we're all expendable!"

Only yesterday, Nolan, Murphy and all the others came face-to-face with the enemy — a large contingent of NVA (North Vietnamese Army Regulars). The Americans consisted of only a small company of grunts from the 3rd Battalion, 7th Infantry of the 199th Infantry Brigade. After the firefight, intelligence estimated that the men were outnumbered more than four to one. The engagement lasted less than twenty minutes, but it was an eternity for those subjected to its horrors. Whizzing bullets flew over their heads, ricocheted off boulders, slammed into trees, and drilled into the sun-baked earth. A number of rounds found their mark.

Soldiers were terrified. A few simply trembled while others stood in shock, none more so than Mullins and Woods who were combat virgins — fuckin' new guys (FNGs) or cherries as they were referred to by other seasoned grunts in the company. Woods had been in country less than ten days and Mullins but a month. For them, this day was to be their baptism by fire, an infantry soldier's sacramental right of passage and one most feared by every cherry that first stepped foot in the land. Despite their stateside training, nothing could have prepared them for the experience they were facing.

During the attack, the tenacious enemy maneuvered with quick precision, taking only minutes to encircle their prey. The makeshift perimeter, haphazardly formed as a defensive maneuver by the Americans, soon began to collapse. Yet, the grunts continued to fight with the ferocity of caged animals, firing their assault rifles on full automatic as they attempted to fend off the determined NVA. Occasionally, a soldier tossed a hand grenade, but it had little, if any, effect in halting the advance. Then, unexpectedly, as if the enemy's plan was designed as a hit-and-run operation, the skirmish ended. At its peak, it was the fiercest and most demonic firefight the men had ever encountered.

It was now dawn. The men were milling around near the staging area, grudgingly contemplating their next assignment. Murphy thought the obvious, being preconditioned to the same eventuality: Here we go again. Another early morning briefing culminating in a quick walk down to the helicopter pad, a harrowing chopper ride to an enemy infested drop-zone, and a deadly firefight in the bush.

The time was 0430. The only illumination in the area was a semi-detached spotlight dangling precariously from a leaning telephone pole as it waved in rhythmic cadence, propelled by a gentle, yet constant, breeze. The light shed from the bulb transmitted an aura of ultra-violet hues through the mist as its rays cascaded downward, barely illuminating the men underneath.

"Can you believe this fog?" Murphy asked.

"Hell . . . It's a bitch!" Nolan replied.

Their deeply carved stress lines rivaled men twice their age. Their eyes were dark and distant as if an abstraction, their skin pallid as if sickly, and, as an Egyptian mummy's, their cheeks hollowed to the bone. Unquestionably, the horrifying effects of their gruesome profession were indelibly etched in their faces. But it didn't end there. What little remained of their sanity was now a scrambled mess of psychological aberrations bearing witness that they had come to understand war in all its shocking cruelty. Nolan and Murphy had long since earned the right to be called combat infantrymen.

Specialist Four Jimmy Rolfe from New York City, standing next to Specialist Four Joseph Kowalczyk, a hard-nosed street kid from the boroughs of Chicago, looked over at his buddy and questioned, "What do ya think this is all about?"

"Who knows?" responded Kowalczyk, as he tried to rub the morning from his eyes. "Damn! I was having this dream about this luscious babe with a face so beautiful that I could hardly look her in the eyes. They better make this good or I'm gonna' be really pissed off."

58

Looking at Kowalczyk, Rolfe laughed and with a smirk on his drawn and thinning face said, "Sure you were. First, you weren't dreaming about her face and, second, that's about as close as you'll ever come to a beautiful woman." With a restrained laugh he drilled Kowalczyk further. "Now what are you going to do about this loss of beauty rest?" Rolfe didn't wait for an answer. His villainous attitude and reputation of being overly condescending was about to become evident. With a stern and sarcastic voice he interjected, "You'll do nothin', not a damn thing. You know it, and so do I!"

Whether Rolfe's assertion was accurate or even deserving a response, Kowalczyk never replied. Exasperated, he gazed at Rolfe but a moment, then blankly stared at the ground.

The early morning sun had yet to rise, and the cold that lingered in the air made the unbearable situation even worse. Soon the grunts expected that the scorching sun — a fact of life in Southeast Asia — would appear and burn off the fog. Since their arrival, the men had learned to coexist with the extremes of early morning cold and unbearably high temperatures in the afternoon, not to mention the other more serious dilemma — not knowing when or where the enemy would strike. No one dared claim they were preconditioned to either of these life-threatening conditions, yet they managed as well as could be expected. For now, it appeared to be just another day of trying to stay alive in a place they best described as hell on earth.

From all indications — the abrupt, early morning wake-up, the gathering of the company at the staging area, and the incessant bitching — another combat briefing was about to take place.

"Fuuuck the army!" an unidentified grunt yelled, his voice echoing in the distance. The message wasn't directed at anyone but only to vent some anger. Soldiers used this technique to cleanse their soul of the military label acquired since taking the oath of allegiance. Few, if any, hated their country. Their gripes concerned the righteousness of the war and what the army molded them into: an efficient, but expendable killing machine. They learned quickly. In a fortnight, they became painfully aware that life in Vietnam was worth less than a '58 Chevy, even one with body rot and blown cylinders.

Nolan heard something stirring in the distance. Turning toward Murphy he said, "What do you make of that?"

Murphy looked up but did not answer. He, too, was puzzled.

Out of the distant fog bank, an obscure figure emerged. As it approached, the men recognized a distinct outline of a man. From what they could ascertain, he was slim, of average height, and ordinary in appearance. Yet, there was something enigmatic about the image that neither could readily identify.

Within thirty yards of the platform, others began to take notice. Soon, all were able to discern the figure. Not long after, the man's face became visible. He was handsome, youthful and without a blemish, as if an artist's model. The sharp outline of his chin complimented his high forehead line, triangular face, and jet-black eyes. The mysterious intruder was dressed in freshly starched jungle fatigues, an ascot, and black combat boots. Wearing nothing on his head, his long black hair appeared unruly. In spite of the fog and semi-darkness, his spit-shined boots were brilliant, as immaculate as the rest of his military attire.

Reaching the stairs, the man hesitated but a second, pausing to look at the sky as if seeking divine intervention. Grabbing the wooden railing, he continued up the stairs and walked toward center stage where a podium had been placed.

After assessing his audience, the man cleared his throat then introduced himself. "Gentlemen! My name is Sergeant Cabral. Please sit down," he said. "It doesn't matter where. Right where you're standing is fine. Quickly, quickly," he said. "We have little time in which to conduct our affairs. Another group is due to arrive shortly."

When the men appeared at ease, Cabral continued. "Each of you has been hand-selected to participate in a extraordinary mission. As for me . . . well . . . I've been ordered to prepare you, the best I can, for the difficult task ahead. But before I do, I must enlighten you on a few details."

Cabral spoke without emotion; his military bearing and meticulous dress hid any trace of an agenda. As stone cold as a sphinx, it soon became evident the sergeant meant nothing but business.

Gathering his thoughts, Cabral told his story. "What happened to me, I wouldn't wish upon my worst enemy. If you will, allow me to explain. I suspect that my experience will help you better understand what all of you will soon encounter."

Back in the audience, Rolfe leaned over and whispered in Kowalczyk's ear, "Sounds like we're in for some serious shit!" Always difficult to assess, there was no way of knowing whether Rolfe was concerned or cynical.

Kowalczyk, looking withdrawn, sensed Rolfe might have been serious as he replied, "Brother, I think you're right! I don't know if I can take another day out in . . . " Kowalczyk was at a loss for words unable to do much more than shake his head in disgust.

Sergeant Cabral continued.

"It would be just another night of guard duty, or so I thought. The date was January 31st. I was stationed at Tan Son Nhut Airbase. Earlier in the evening of the 30th, it was brutally hot, but by nightfall, the heat and stifling humidity had lessened considerably."

Sergeant Cabral Delivers a Somber Message

"We had never experienced combat before — not Davidson, not McLaughlin, not Miller nor Diaz. Not any of us," Cabral confessed. "Heck, we were in the Air Force. We chose this branch because of its well-earned reputation of being the least risky of all the services."

In the audience, Sergeant John Peters poked Rolfe's arm to get his attention. When Rolfe acknowledged with a simple nod, Peters leaned over and whispered in Rolfe's ear: "Why are we listening to this swill?" followed by, "Who the hell wants to hear this guy's sob story? I've got enough problems to worry about."

"Fuckin-A, man!" Rolfe concurred.

Cabral overheard the conversation but made no attempt at admonishment. He had performed his duties too many times and knew how to address such an interruption. Looking at the entire group, he said, "If any of you think there isn't a purpose to my story, let me see a show of hands." There were no takers. As for Peters, he looked aghast that Cabral had overheard his smart-ass remark.

"Getting back to my story," Cabral said, as he tightly gripped both sides of the lectern with each hand. Perhaps it gave him more support, but probably was only a gesture intended to show his resolve. "I was assigned bunker duty as an Air Force security guard at the western end of the perimeter. With me were four other guys from my unit. I remember Diaz looking at his watch. The time was 0230. Looking into the distance, we could see movement." With these words, Cabral became more animated, but still concealed any hint of genuine emotion. "Several times we radioed the information back to headquarters, and each time we were told not to break radio silence unless our lives were in imminent danger. Suddenly, without warning, we were attacked by an enemy, a foe who possessed a ground force of overwhelming odds. Before long, several rounds fired from a rocket-propelled grenade launcher hit our bunker. In the end, only one of us survived."

"Gentlemen, this concludes the main part of my briefing," Cabral said as he stepped back from the podium, still maintaining the same expressionless face as when he first spoke.

The men appeared bewildered at the bizarre and abrupt way Cabral concluded his story. Others were delighted as they thought his message peculiar and without merit.

"Thank God!" Rolfe muttered to Kowalczyk. "What the hell was that all about?"

Before other derogatory comments could be made, Cabral again approached the podium. The voices quieted down, but a few were still talking when Cabral began to speak.

"Now, gentlemen," he continued, "this brings me to the most important segment of my briefing. I am commanded to show you something that will disturb you. What you will see will be troublesome to watch!" Speaking in a commanding voice, he said, "Look! Look out there in the distance!"

He pointed to an area where the fog had all but evaporated. As his words were spoken, an inconceivable scene became visible at ground level. A break in the fog exposed a slow-moving vortex that was spinning counter-clockwise. To the men, the view was hazy — opaque and surreal, different than looking at a movie on the big screen, yet clear enough to see detailed images.

"Pay close attention" Cabral said, "because the significance of what you're about to see will soon become apparent."

Gradually, a scene of total and utter chaos unfolded before their eyes. Watching the vision, the men appeared confused and dumbfounded. It wasn't long before they realized that this was their company, the 3rd Battalion, 7th Infantry, and it was a scene mysteriously replicated from yesterday's firefight.

"How can this be happening?" Fernandez murmured.

Nolan, Murphy, O'Neil, Peters and many others sat upright, mouths ajar, displaying expressions of profound disbelief.

In the vision, the enemy was everywhere. Within minutes the skirmish had degenerated into a life-threatening encounter of grenade throwing and hand-to-hand combat. The Americans were taking a terrible beating.

Sounds were heard, and they were every bit as ugly as the images that had first appeared. Crazed and frantic, a man screamed, "They're all over the place. What should we do?"

An officer barked a command: "Watch out for your left flank."

"Medic . . . medic! I'm hit!" shouted a wounded soldier.

Another man, sensing the inevitable, yelled, "Holy shit. We're being overrun!"

"I'm calling in air support," hollered the officer.

A soldier, shot through the neck, lay paralyzed and dying. Screaming in distress, he pleaded, "Please help me . . . I can't feel my legs! God, please don't let me die!" The medic was unable to assist. He was tending to another GI with a gunshot wound to the head.

Murphy recognized himself immediately. Falling, face first to the ground, he suffered horrendous fragmentation wounds to the head, face, arms, and chest. His left arm was torn from its shoulder socket, twisted in the opposite direction from which it belonged. As his body tumbled to the ground, he lay motionless, slumped near a small boulder. Witnessing the carnage, all he could do was gasp in disbelief.

Fernandez gazed at the illusion not wanting to believe his eyes. "Ssshhhit!" he exclaimed, as he watched himself being struck by a bullet fired from pointblank range. His chest exploded as the round exited his body carrying with it blood, rib fragments, muscle, flesh, and torn fragments of his fatigue jacket. It appeared as spray being ejected from an aerosol can, only this liquid consisted of minute amounts of blood, body fluids, and other gruesome residue from his chest and disemboweled abdomen. The high velocity at impact threw him forward and slammed him to the ground. He rolled onto his right side as his body convulsed in rapid succession. In slow motion, he curled into a fetal position, shook for a final time, and then lay motionless.

Soon, others bore witness to a similar fate — an un-predictable and abominable termination to their earthly existence. During fierce hand-to-hand combat, the soldiers watched as they were struck by bullets, fragmented by grenades, or stabbed by the enemy.

As quickly as the vision appeared, so too did it disappear into the haze and fog that surrounded the area. Only a tranquil scene remained as if nothing out of the ordinary had happened.

After the vision evaporated, Cabral turned toward the stunned and frightened men. Taking a few moments to gather his thoughts, he broke the uneasy silence. "What you have just seen is true. It is an uncensored account of what happened to all of you yesterday."

Meanwhile, Rolfe, always a doubting Thomas, found it difficult to accept the proceedings. Recalcitrant and contemptuous, he waited as a lion stocking its prey for an opportune moment to pounce.

"That brings me to the main reason why I'm here today," Cabral continued. "I have been assigned by a higher command to act as your transition counselor. Like you, I have come from the wilderness of the battlefield. Hear what I have to say, and your walk will be brief and rewarding." With his choice of words, Cabral sounded more like a preacher than a sergeant in the military.

"You have been summoned for final out-processing. Soon, the war as you know it will no longer be of concern. Presently, you are at a way station, a safe haven through which all mankind must pass. You are here . . . because you are no longer among the living."

The phantasmagoric had now become shocking reality as evidenced by the bewildered expression on the men's faces, that is, all but Rolfe who blurted out in anger, "What, in the name of God, is that crazed asshole talkin' about?"

Kowalczyk, too, was irritated, but for a different reason. Using the same inflection in his voice that Rolfe employed on him, he said, "Rolfe! If somebody hit you between the eyes with a friggin' two-by-four, you still wouldn't get it? For the love of God, man, don't you understand? You're dead . . . he's dead . . . we're all dead! Rolfe! Let me be the first to tell you. You're a friggin' idiot. Now shut the hell up!"

Rarely spoken to in such a manner, Rolfe was stunned. For the moment, he was silenced.

From the podium, Cabral looked at Kowalczyk. Perhaps he was pleased at Kowalczyk's percipient nature and how he handled Rolfe's disruption, although it wasn't evident in his eyes. There was still that vacant stare, a strange mysterious gaze devoid of any compassion or humanity. Waiting but a second, Cabral turned toward the men and returned to business.

"Gentlemen. I have something else to reveal. I, too, was killed in battle. It was during Tet of '68. As for the story I just conveyed, I was not the survivor."

Frightened beyond belief, the men did little more than listen. There were a few skeptics, and Cabral sensed this, but he also realized that time would be the convincing factor and play in his favor.

"Soon you will meet others much like yourselves. In consideration of your noble sacrifice, you have been granted a quick and safe passage into a glorious new world. Soon you will transcend your earthly bodies and journey to a place few thought possible. For the first time, you will experience inner peace, as absolute as bright stars in the heavens. Your journey will take you to a world where joy and love know no bounds, where you have no enemies, and peace lasts an eternity."

Looking out from the podium, Cabral noticed several men squirming. Some covered their faces and wept. A few cried uncontrollably, making no pretence to hide their grief. Emotions such as these were nothing new to him.

As the fog gradually lifted, a panorama of stark and shocking reality surfaced: those in the assembly were wearing bloodstained uniforms. Their fatigues were badly soiled and jaggedly torn. Many of the decrepit figures were partially naked; their horrendous wounds visible for all to see. Every single soldier was a casualty of war. There were no wounded, only the dead.

Rolfe sprang up from the ground, tore off what little remained of his blood-soaked t-shirt, and observed a wound in his chest that would kill a horse. "My God!" he blurted out as he fell to his knees. Overwhelmed and unable to make sense of his predicament, Rolfe's sense of humor and condescending personality completely eluded him. Others followed suit ripping off their fatigues, all looking for an apparent death wound.

Private Woods, one of the FNGs, had stripped himself naked in an unsuccessful attempt to find his. Maddeningly, he yelled: "I don't belong here, 'cause I haven't been hit! I know I'm not dead! God, please get me out of here!"

Nolan, standing directly behind him, put his search to rest.

Looking at the poor soul, he said, "Put your hand behind your head."

Reluctantly, Woods complied as he took his right hand and placed it directly below the back of his bush hat. What he felt or did not feel was unnerving. There was little remaining to the back of his skull. A round from an AK-47 Russian assault rifle had struck him squarely behind his left ear. The bullet had exited through the back of the head, ripping out large chunks of brain matter and skull fragments.

Sergeant Cabral, sensing the soldiers' extreme discomfort and psychological frailty, quickly intervened. "Not to worry, gentlemen! Soon you will depart this place and leave what is left of your earthly remains. Only your soul will journey forward. Where you're going, your earthly bodies will be a hindrance." His words were comforting, and appeased the disbelief of several of the men.

"What is it like to be dead?" Cabral asked, anticipating the inevitable question not yet voiced. He answered succinctly. "Actually, I never felt dead. Even now, I feel more alive than ever before." He continued. "Death is not easy to accept, but for that matter, neither is life. It didn't take long before I came to accept my fate, and so, too, will you. Besides, the rewards are far greater where you'll be traveling than on earth." Cabral thought for a second and added: "Gentlemen. I am at peace."

He knew his answer would not suffice, at least in the immediate future. There were things best left for the men to experience on their own.

"Each of you has been assigned a mentor who will counsel and comfort you. You see it's good to talk about what happened. There is therapy for the mind, and there is therapy for the soul. Here we concentrate on the latter."

"Now," Cabral asked, "are there any questions?"

"Will I need any supplies or equipment?" asked a nervous Private Olsen.

"You stupid idiot," interjected a soldier sitting directly across from him. "You're dead. What the hell would you do with 'em, even if you had 'em?"

Cabral did not answer. Olsen sensed the answer almost the same time he asked the question.

"Why us? Why did God kill us?" shouted a soldier sitting a distance from the podium.

"God does not kill man; man kills man!" exclaimed Cabral. "God is more appalled than you at these unconscionable acts of violence inflicted upon His loving creations."

Another soldier who had been crying since Cabral's initial disclosure tried to hold back the tears long enough to ask, "What about my Mom and Dad? Will I ever see them again?"

Cabral faced this question more times than he cared to remember, and answering it never got easier as there was nothing he knew to appease a man's anxiety or pacify his curiosity during the early transition stages of death to eternal life. Regardless, Cabral made an attempt. Looking at the young man, he asked, "What is your name, soldier?"

"Corporal James Kirkland, Sergeant," the soldier answered, sobbing all the while.

Not showing even the slightest bit of remorse, Cabral answered, "Mothers, fathers, sisters, brothers and all your other relatives and friends will soon mourn your passing. With great difficulty they will continue on with their lives. But someday soon they, too, will be called. When their day arrives, you will meet them again. But for now, you are paving their way just as many others have laid the foundation for you."

As Cabral continued to take more questions, several men dressed in varied military attire walked through the fog bank toward the podium. Their uniforms were ragged, bloodied, and soiled. These casualties, which no longer bordered an illusion, represented ill-fated participants from almost every major war: a Roman naval hero who fought in the First Punic War and gave his life on a small, desolate island off the coast of Sicily; a medieval horseman, fully clad in body armour, from the days of the

Crusades, killed by Turkish forces; and, a Confederate sharpshooter from America's Civil War, dressed in slouch-hat and homemade, chestnut-dyed attire, who sacrificed his life for a losing cause at Antietam. Following closely behind was a Sioux Indian, a scout who fought and died at Little Big Horn; a young World War I soldier, wearing a tight-fitting, dough-boy uniform, who was laid to rest near Verdun; and an elderly German soldier from World War II, still wearing an Iron Cross around his neck, who was killed in the Motherland during the final defensive campaign of the Third Reich. There was even an American grunt from the Vietnam War, wearing the same faded jungle fatigues he was killed in after the Viet Cong ambushed his convoy on the An Khe Pass. In the background, another twelve to fifteen soldiers advanced toward the podium.

"Those you see walking toward you," Cabral elaborated, "will aid you in understanding your journey and offer comfort along the way. You see them in their human forms just as they would have looked on earth. Yet, they are souls just like me and soon what you will become. Hear me. Each of you will be assigned a counselor, a guide if you will, who will help you transcend your bodies. But first, as I speak, you will lose all sense of human emotion."

No sooner did the words leave his lips then each man felt a strange sensation. Not emotional, the transformation was heavenly, one of complete bliss, unlike anything each had ever experienced while alive.

Within seconds, the fog disappeared from view leaving a rainbow of brilliant hues. The recently ordained spirits stood and gazed in awe at its breathtaking and supernatural beauty. Mysteriously, the ground beneath their feet became invisible. As the intensity of the colors encircled and enshrouded them, each soul became suspended in time.

In succession, a guide walked up to a soldier. First, the Confederate sharpshooter approached Kirkland and, in a gesture of compassion, lightly grasped his hand. Next came the old German warrior, followed closely by the others. Several extended their right hand in friendship. Others placed an arm around the newcomers' back. As if in a procession, each pair walked toward the vortex that had suddenly reappeared, gliding as if riding on an invisible cloud. Slowly, the guides and soldiers disappeared into the heavens; a universe that gently melded into breathtaking colors and far expanses of space.

After the soldiers departed, Cabral stood alone at the podium. Looking up, he gazed at the heavens as an astronomer would. A slight grin appeared on his face. Slowly, his image began to blur as it became evanescent before totally disappearing from view.

Only moments passed before the dazzling array of colors faded to darkness.

It could have been minutes, perhaps hours, maybe even days, but the sky eventually lightened. Fog gently rolled in. Without warning, the perfect silence was shattered by a voice emanating from the distance:

"Why are they waking us up so early?"

"Damned if I know!" a soldier replied. "I'd rather be dead than to have to go out on another patrol!"

IN THE BUSH

People will insist...on treating the mons Veneris
as though it were Mount Everest.
-Aldous Huxley, *Eyeless in Gaza* (1936)

"**M**arv, this ain't any bullshit. Honest . . . it's not! If I hadn't of seen it with my own two eyes, I wouldn't have believed it myself."

"What are ya talkin' about?" Marv asked.

"Yesterday, down at the airfield a flight mechanic showed me this magazine. Said he bought it from an FNG who just flew in from the World."

"So, what was so special about it?" Marv questioned.

In dramatic detail, Alan explained all his reasons to Marv. Before he concluded he added, "Cost him fifteen bucks. Hell. I wouldn't have paid more than five!"

"Yeah, right!" said Marv with a tinge of sarcasm.

Marv's demeanor caught Alan off guard.

"Really! I think he got a royal screwin'. Think about it. Once the mail arrives everyone with a subscription will have his own copy."

"I suppose," Marv said although disinclined to agree; "but you're forgettin' one important detail."

"And what's that?" Alan asked.

"At least he's the first guy on the block to have a copy. You know what that means, don't you?"

"No."

"It means he's got braggin' rights."

"Sure he does, but for how long?" Alan said as he tried valiantly to defend his position.

Marv needed little time to think of a reply as he answered, "Long enough to squeeze all the mileage that he can out of it!" Pleased with his retort, Marv wore a sneer from ear-to-ear. He continued: "Ya know, perhaps that saying is true after all."

"I'm almost afraid to ask. What saying?"

Marv peered at Alan and with the same arrogant grin responded; "'A bird in the hand is worth two in the bush.'"

"Very funny, Marv. You're a real friggin' comedian, you are."

After Marv stopped laughing, he gathered his composure long enough to ask a question. "By the way, how'd you run into this guy?"

Alan answered without hesitation.

"I was dropping off some papers for the colonel — documents that had to be on the afternoon shuttle for Saigon, when I bumped into him in the main terminal as he was coming out the front door. I was walking in. Neither of us was paying much attention, and we slammed right into each other."

"I suppose after your collision, he just showed you the damn magazine?"

"Well . . . yeah, that's kinda what happened," Alan said. "He had it rolled up in one of his hands so you couldn't see the cover. Let me tell you! He was holding onto that magazine for dear life like it was a national treasure or somethin'. Without warning, he opened it to the foldout section and spread it before my eyes. 'Hey, brother! Get a load of this!' I think he said. Well . . . let me tell you. I was speechless; blown away is more like it. There it was in all its honored glory unveiled right before my virgin eyes."

Alan lingered over the thought for some time before Marv brought him back to his senses.

"Well, Sergeant Virgin! What did it look like?"

"It's hard for me to describe. You had to have been there for yourself. But I'll say one thing. It was exquisite; an absolute thing of beauty," Alan said proudly. "Listen," he continued. "My copy should be arriving any day. When I get it, you'll be the first I'll show it to."

"Promise?"

"I promise."

"Thanks, man!" Marv had all he could do to contain his lascivious grin.

An announcement came over the company loudspeaker almost a week to the day that Alan told Marv about his fortunate encounter with the flyboy.

"MAIL CALL!"

It wasn't long before Alan, Marv, and just about everyone else in the company made a mad dash down to the mailroom.

"Maybe today's the day," Alan told Marv.

"I sure hope so," Marv said, a bit winded from the jog.

"Look at the guy's bag," Alan said.

"Why?" Before Alan could answer, Marv noticed a number of sleeved envelopes protruding from the mail clerk's pouch.

"Bailey!" shouted the mail clerk.

"Here!" Bailey yelled as he made his way to the front of the line only to have several letters handed to him. He waited a bit longer, but nothing else came his way. He looked dismayed.

"Cunningham!"

"Right here," said the soldier standing but a few feet away from the mail clerk. Cunningham was luckier. His surprise had arrived along with a few letters from home. Quickly, he disappeared into the inner-sanctum of his tent.

Alan's surname was Tomlinson. Marv waited patiently as the mail was handed out alphabetically. The suspense was killing Marv. For him, it seemed like an eternity before the mail clerk was calling the 'T's.' Alan was the third of the 'T's' to be called.

Finally, the mail clerk called Alan's last name: "Tomlinson!"

"Here. I'm coming through," he said. Reaching the front, he reached over the shoulder of one man and extended his right hand. The mail clerk placed three letters in his hand then a plain, brown-sleeved envelope. Alan walked to the rear of the pack where Marv was waiting anxiously. Bending the envelope ever so slightly with his hands, Alan was able to see the glorious treasure that lay inside. The title was easily discernible: *PLAYBOY*.

"Rip off the wrapper, for Christ sake, and let me see," Marv said.

"Once we get inside the tent," Alan replied. "You waited a week, Marv, so what's another minute."

"To me . . . an eternity. Come on, Alan. Let's get out of here."

"Don't you even want to see if ya got any mail?"

Marv answered without giving it a thought. "I'll pick it up tomorrow." Marv's last name was Zimmermann.

Arriving at their destination, Alan handed the envelope to his friend. It didn't take Marv long to tear off the wrapper and open the magazine to the centerfold. There was no mistaking what he saw.

"Holy cow!" Marv said. "Will you look at this? It's pubic hair all right."

"I told you," Alan said. Marv didn't appear to hear him.

Odd, Marv thought: The hair on her head is much lighter. He continued to peruse the centerfold the same way a forensic scientist examines a minute amount of evidence — deliberately and with the scrutiny of a Sherlock Holmes-schooled detective. The only article lacking for a more thorough investigation was a magnifying glass. If he had one, he would have used it to his advantage.

Although not the first issue to show pubic hair — the August 1972 issue featuring model Liv Lindeland from Norway as the 'Playmate of the Month' would claim the illustrious distinction of being the first reputable men's magazine to display a frontal view while exposing a significant area of the lower anatomy. The pictorial layout was tastefully presented, though prudes would argue the contrary. An attractive and amply endowed Miss August 1972 was lying on her left side in the sand on a pink blanket wearing nothing but her birthday suit.

"Well! What do you think?" Alan asked, although he already surmised Marv's response.

"Incredible! Absolutely indescribably incredible!"

For the next few minutes, nothing was said. While Alan read a letter from home, Marv gawked at the centerfold, examining it from every conceivable angle.

Finally Alan caught Marv's attention when he said, "For Christ sake, you're going to wear out the damn page. Take a break. Check out the back section while you're at it." Having seen the magazine a week previous, Alan was well aware that his friend was in for another treat, but he didn't want to spoil the surprise.

Marv found it difficult to remove his lustful eyes from the page, but he did manage to look up long enough to ask, what he though was, an intelligent question: "Why?"

"You'll see!"

Marv complied, although reluctantly. Flipping through several pages he came upon a photo essay titled The Girls of Munich. "Fuuuck me!" he exclaimed

The Fräuleins of Germany added even more icing to an already delicious cake. Several maidens — well, maybe not maidens by strict definition — were frolicking naked as jaybirds in outdoor settings (woods and city streets). As for the pièce de résistance: nearly every female revealed her pubic hair in her photo layout. The last bastion of censorship had fallen, not once but several times. The August 1972 *Playboy* was an issue every young soldier would have fought over and, most likely, would have done so with reckless abandon.

The tantalizing and revealing photos were more than Marv could stand — literally. With sweaty palms and flushed face, he leaned against the center tent pole for support and said out load, "I wish I was back in the States."

Alan laughed at Marv's comment although he, too, felt the same. "Now do you understand why the guy paid fifteen bucks for the magazine?"

Sheepishly, Marv shook his head and said, "Now I do."

The Plain Brown Wrapper

RE-EVALUATING NEWTON'S
LAW OF GRAVITY

Wild animals never kill for sport. Man is the only one to whom the torture and death of his fellow creatures is amusing in itself.
-James A. Froude, *Oceana* (1886)

Rational beings would argue that in a country at war there'd be little opportunity to re-test an already well-established, scientific principle, or so a person would imagine. Yet, amazingly, that's exactly what happened.

In 1684, English physicist Sir Isaac Newton formulated the first theory of gravity. According to Newton, "The gravitational attraction between two bodies is directly proportional to the product of the masses of the two bodies and inversely proportional to the square of the distance between them." Years later, and on numerous occasions, scientists reconfirmed the theory. As they all learned, because the earth is in a constant state of motion, gravitational forces are lessened by centrifugal force, which counteracts and lessens the gravitational effect. Because centrifugal force is greater at the equator than it is at the poles, the speed of a falling object is slightly less in places like Vietnam, which is closer to the equator than it would be at either the North or South Poles. Still sound confusing? Think of it in these simplistic terms: because earth contains a dense atmosphere, what goes up, must come down. And the closer someone gets to the equator, the slower an object will descend from the sky.

"Mosley!"

"Yes, First Sergeant."

"How long have ya been in 'Nam?"

"About seven months," Adam replied.

"I figured that long," Waterson said, continuing to chomp on his half-lit cigar. "I've got some news for you, Mosley."

"What's that?" Adam asked.

"You've being reassigned to an ARVN helicopter unit. You gonna be their advisor."

"Damn!" Adam said.

Waterson laughed. "Man, some guys get all the choice assignments. Don't be reticent, Mosley. Shit happens. Look at it as a vacation. Where else but in 'Nam could you get such an opportunity. Best of all, you'll be able to mingle with the Vietnamese Nationals, learn their culture, and eat all of their delicious food."

"Damn . . . damn . . . damn!" Adam said. With a sour expression that gave every indication he sucked on a lemon and, worse, swallowed the seeds, he was far from delighted. Prior to his new assignment, Adam served as an infantry soldier. As an 11 Bravo, he took part in, what many GIs called, The Native Sport — hunting Viet Cong and North Vietnam Army Regulars. While an infantryman, he quickly learned that ARVNs were unreliable, unpatriotic, and in far too many instances, card-carrying cowards. After he was hit — not a million-dollar wound — he was assigned to the 12th Psychological Operations Group not far from Pleiku in the Central Highlands. Adam's primary mission was to assist with psychological operations and act as a technical liaison to the ARVN's. In this capacity, he wrote propaganda leaflets later to be dropped over select hamlets populated by communist sympathizers, prepared radio and television propaganda broadcasts, conducted mobile radio surveillance, and performed operations research. Until that time, Adam's interface with the ARVNs was only on a small scale.

First Sergeant Waterson wouldn't let go. "Mosley! I've heard there's some pretty strange happenings goin' on in that unit."

"Like what, First Sergeant?"

"I'm not sure I believe what I heard, kid, but if I were you, I'd re-read your Geneva Convention Card just to be on the safe side."

"My what?" Adam quizzed.

"Your Geneva Convention Card. Remember all the stuff they gave you with your orders when you left Long Binh for reassignment into the field?"

"Kind of," Adam replied, offering a less than enthusiastic response.

"Well I suggest if you do nothin' else tonight, you read that card."

Waterson had better things to do. He turned and walked away.

Late that evening, after digging through mounds of paperwork, Adam found the wallet-size card. It was in a small, brown shoebox underneath his bunk. Opening the four-page, double-spaced card, he read it:

As a member of the US Military Forces, you will comply with the Geneva Prisoner of War Conventions of 1949 to which your country adheres. Under these conventions: you can and will disarm your prisoner; immediately search him thoroughly; require him to be silent; segregate him from other prisoners; guard him carefully; and, take him to the place designated by your commander.

There was more.

You cannot and must not mistreat your prisoner; humiliate or degrade him; take any of his personal effects, which do not have significant military value; and, refuse him medical treatment if required and available.

The last sentence bluntly declared:

Always treat your prisoner humanely.

Now why in hell would the First Sergeant want me to read this, he thought? I'm being assigned as an advisor to a helicopter crew, not a prisoner interrogation unit.

Days later, Adam found himself mingling with the South Vietnamese helicopter crew at the landing pad. From what he learned earlier in the morning, the men he would be working alongside were former members of the ARVN, 2nd Ranger Group, 4th Armor Brigade and the 7th Ranger Group, 5th Armor Brigade. Adam reflected: Maybe I shouldn't prejudge. After all, they were infantry rangers, even if only ARVNs. It wasn't long before Adam learned this was not your typical ARVN helicopter unit. He was being assigned to an ARVN command whose sole responsibility was breaking-down Viet Cong prisoners. But why a helicopter unit?, he wondered over and over.

For nearly 300 years, Newton's Law of Gravity was accepted as an irrefutable scientific fact. Why would anyone ever need to retest the theory?

One afternoon after interrogating prisoners in the conventional manner, an ARVN officer conceived, what he thought, a brilliant idea. His name was Captain Đinh. Captain Đinh came from an affluent and distinguished family. Rumors abounded that in the early sixties his father sent him abroad to study at a large mid-western university in the States. Supposedly, he graduated with a degree in physics. His college background was never substantiated. Adam soon learned several distinct characteristics set Đinh apart from his counterparts: his command of the English language, his warped sense of humor, and his sadistic personality.

With his newly acquired knowledge and predilection for the macabre, Đinh was selected as the successor to a Vietnamese captain recently reassigned back to the bush. No one questioned why. The previous commander was having difficulty making a parrot talk, never mind the enemy.

Early that late-August afternoon, just before the monsoons, Đinh entertained his brainstorm. If the previous commander had difficulty extracting credible information from the enemy while on level ground, why not conduct the interrogation in flight. No one doubted that this method would bring an air of mystery to the process.

Applying his knowledge of the physical sciences, Đinh formulated two hypotheses. Neither required an understanding of differential equations or integral calculus. He stated each as a question. The first hypotheses had a direct correlation to Newton's Law of Gravity:

Does a human fall to earth faster in Vietnam than he would in Antarctica?

81

The second was his own unique theory, one that would be much easier to prove or discount: Can VC fly?

Captain Đinh became a soul possessed. To re-test the first theory and substantiate the second, Đinh followed the scientific method. He was adamant about doing it right. Đinh set three objectives as a goal. The first was to prove or disprove his scientific theories. The second was to validate his worth as a chief interrogator and as a helicopter squadron leader, and the third, to inflict his ghastly revenge upon the enemy.

Captain Đinh wasn't always over the edge as Adam soon learned. When only a boy of 12, he was forced to witness the execution of his father by the Viet Cong. The papa-san was accused of collaborating with an American army colonel about the identification of suspected VC sympathizers. True or not, his father paid dearly. During the incident, the VC savagely raped and beat his mother and sister. The assault was so fiendish that neither would fully recover. Later in the day, the VC reduced the village to rubble. Though physically spared, Đinh would never forget. He swore that as long as he lived, the killing of his father and the rapes of his mother and sister would be avenged.

"You will fly with us for the first time," Đinh said to Adam.

"Yes, Sir," Adam replied.

"Pay close attention, Sergeant," Captain Đinh said. "You will learn something today."

"I will, Sir?" Adam said.

"Yes, you will," Captain Đinh answered.

Taking great pains to ensure that the experiments would not be compromised, the prisoners were blindfolded before boarding the helicopter.

"Where are we taking them, Sir? Adam asked.

"In the sky," Captain Đinh said.

"I know that, Sir, but . . . I mean . . . to what base?"

Captain Đinh looked at Adam as a veteran football player would peer at a rookie during his first day of training camp.

"There is no other base. It will be a one-way trip."

Mosley looked confused. Gathering his thoughts, he asked, "Why, then, are we taking them for a ride, Sir?"

"Pay attention, Sergeant. You will soon learn the proper technique in breaking prisoners."

Adam sat back and reflected: *What the hell is this guy talking about?*

While in the air, not even the ARVN crewmembers were allowed to speak to the prisoners. After flying to a height of about 7,500 feet, Đinh removed the blindfolds while his men continued to restrain the prisoners. The fear that registered in the eyes of the alleged VC was nothing less than sheer terror. Đinh's conducted his interrogation in both Vietnamese and English. It helped that Adam was trained at an army linguist school back in the States. Although, certainly not fluent in Vietnamese, he understood most conversations. Now, all he could do was watch and listen.

"Are you VC?"

"*Tôi không hiều.*" (I don't understand.)

"*Anh có phài VC không?*" (Are you VC?)

"*Tôi không phài VC.*" (Me no VC.)

" *Tôi hòi lai. Anh có phài VC không?*" (I ask again. Are you VC?)

" *Tôi không phài VC!*" (Me no VC!)

"*Dù rồi! Đú rồi! Anh là VC!*" (Enough! Enough! You are VC!)

"*Không phài VC! Không phài VC!*" (No VC! No VC!)

Within fifteen seconds, Captain Đinh would ask the same question a final time: "*Anh cô VC?*"

"*Câm! Câm!*" was the usual reply.

Though frightened, Adam doubted any prisoner believed his life was in imminent danger. At worst, he suspected each expected a beating, certainly nothing more drastic.

Near the end of the interrogation, Captain Đinh lost patience. Adam thought: *Maybe it's all a ploy to legitimize his cruel game.*

Reconciling within his own soul that he had done all possible to elicit a confession from the prisoners, Đinh signaled his men to push the first prisoner toward the open door. Adam watched in horror as the prisoner left rubber heel marks from his Ho Chi Minh sandals on the deck plate while trying to avoid certain death. With

83

his right hand clenched and his thumb extended, Đinh pointed over his right shoulder at the door. "Bon Voyage," he said. As if rehearsed, the ARVN's proceeded to throw the prisoner out the chopper door.

"Holy shit," Adam said, not wanting to believe what he had witnessed.

It wasn't over. The pilot rapidly descended and maneuvered the chopper so that all aboard could watch the prisoner's descent. It wasn't pretty. As Adam peered out the door, he didn't see the VC fly. Nevertheless, the test subject seemed to make a concerted effort to do just that. The flight, if you could call it that, resembled a wounded duck failing to maintain sufficient altitude. The freefall lasted but a minute; as the body somersaulted, the arms flailed, and the legs kicked in every conceivable direction. Within 500 feet of the ground, the pilot slowed the chopper's decent, hovered several seconds and departed but only after all aboard witnessed the culmination of the sad event. Forty-five seconds after reaching terminal velocity, the body instantly compressed after hitting the ground. From what Adam could see, the remains were unrecognizable as a human being . . . nothing but mush.

Understandably, it wasn't long before the other prisoners, eyes bulging from their sockets and shaking like a bowl of Jell-O, began confessing their sins.

"Now, Sergeant. Do you understand how we make VC talk?"

Sergeant Mosley was in shock. All he could do was shake his head in the affirmative.

Captain Đinh grinned.

Whether Newton's Law of Gravity was ever corroborated during the war, no one knows for sure. Yet there are those who swore it had. During his final assignment, Adam never did see crewmembers timing the descent of a VC with a stopwatch. But even if he had, there were far too many variables: things like altitude, wind speed, forces of resistance, and trajectory. Furthermore, no one established a valid baseline upon which to measure the findings. After all, who in his right mind would fly a chopper to Antarctica to time a similar descent and then return to

Vietnam to make a comparison? Regardless, and as Adam came to learn, nothing ever discouraged the crew from throwing out an occasional VC prisoner or two.

Captain Đinh was still in command when Adam's tour came to an end. At the time, there were rumblings that an American Inspector General was investigating Đinh's experiments. Happy to be over with the whole bloody mess and pleased he never took part in any of the experiments, Adam said good-bye to the flight crew. There was a final encounter with Captain Đinh. Adam saw him standing on the helicopter tarmac just before catching his chopper back to Cam Ranh Bay, a prelude to his Freedom Bird home. As best as he recollected, it was the first time Captain Đinh ever opened up to him.

"A thousand deaths would never repay what my family experienced at the hands of the VC, nor would a thousand more," Đinh said. There was no doubt in Adam's mind that Captain Đinh was candid and sincere. Looking Adam straight in the eyes, he asked a question, which, even until this day, still

throws Adam for a loop. For some strange reason, Adam figured that if someone believed they were crazy, they probably weren't. If they thought themselves sane, they probably were crazy.

"Do you think I am insane?" Đinh said.

That's all Adam needed to hear to begin questioning his own opinion about the man. "Certainly not, Captain!" came Adam's response, but he wasn't sure he believed what he had just said.

"You are not being honest, my friend! Your eyes betray you!"

There wasn't much Adam could say. Self-consciously, he tried not to make further eye contact during the remainder of the conversation.

"Don't worry," Đinh said. "Even my own men think I am, and maybe they are right!" Placing his right hand over his heart as if making a pledge, he said, "Never, ever will my thirst for enemy blood lessen! I know that I will not survive this war. I beg of you. After you go home, let your people know what is happening here. Tell them the VC killed our families and destroyed our homes. Tell them we are good people driven to madness by the enemy. Tell them we will resist until the end. But above all . . . tell them we will need the continued support of our American friends to succeed." Đinh's words were prophetic even though Adam never realized it at the time — not that he could have done anything about it. "I will pass your message along," Adam said without reservation.

Before departing, Captain Đinh wished Adam a safe trip: "*Chúc ông di bình yên.*"

In English, Adam said, "Good-bye!"

"*Chào!*" Đinh said in return.

As Captain Đinh turned to leave on his way to interrogate another group of Viet Cong, Adam heard him mumble something in Vietnamese.

"*Vâng. Khộng khi tư'o'i rất tốt cho các tù nhân.*"

Roughly translated, Adam thought he said, "Yes. The fresh air will do the prisoners good."

Adam Mosley had read the newspaper and magazine accounts, seen the ghastly images on TV, and viewed the photographs on the Internet. To him, the alleged incidents at Abu Ghraib Prison in Iraq were far from shocking. Heck, he had lived it for several months during his tour of duty. Although it wasn't American soldiers who committed the atrocities, they were still crimes: crimes against humanity. Adam never was questioned about what he saw in Vietnam nor did he ever divulge his dark secret. That made it even more unbearable. The grisly scenes Adam witnessed some thirty-five years ago provided him a constant reminder: that man, by his sheer existence, retains the unenviable trait for committing violent acts, much of which is practiced with little, if any, guilt. He is, by far, the cruelest and most sadistic of all God's creations.

For the rest of his life, Adam would be haunted by Captain Đinh's words:

"Yes. The fresh air will do the prisoners good."

**A Latter-Day Isaac Newton
Contemplates His Latest Experiment**

LADY

A t first glance, having the added responsibility of caring for a dog while serving in a combat zone appeared to be a questionable decision, especially when considering Chuck Newell's military occupation — an infantryman. On the contrary, it proved to be far less demanding than first imagined. Caring for a dog liberated Chuck from the trepidation and misfortunes of war and the everyday doldrums of camp life. What's more, his personal commitment to care for an animal reinforced something he thought he had lost; the God-given capacity for love, to love in an irrational world surrounded by so much hate and discontent in a place devoid of reason and humanity.

Love was an inaccessible commodity for men at war. For Chuck, it was the opposite, even though it was only a dog's affection.

"Will you get a load of that?" Sal said.

Chuck turned to see a small, emaciated dog, perhaps no older than two or three, wandering into the compound. "Well, I'll be damned," he said. "Where do you think that thing is headed?"

"My guess would be the dump," Sal said.

The dump was nothing more than a garbage heap, ripe with the foulest odors. The relentless rays of the sun made it even more repulsive. In a day or two, a GI would be pouring gasoline over the pile of waste and setting it on fire.

Chuck was concerned. "Looks like the mutt hasn't eaten in days." Looking closer, he said, "I think it's female."

The dog's mission that day was one of basic necessity. She was starving to death and wantonly scavenging for any kind of sustenance to maintain what little strength she could muster. It was anyone's guess when, if ever, she ate a nutritious meal. Skin and bones was all she was; ironically, a physical condition which likely prolonged her life. Ten pounds heavier and she could have turned into a Vietnamese gastronomical delicacy.

"I'm gonna try to get closer," Chuck said.

"Why?" asked Sal.

"I don't know. I guess I just feel bad to see an animal in that kinda condition."

As Chuck approached for a closer look at the grungy, shorthaired, oyster-white mutt, he could see she was even more neglected than first imagined. Hundreds of fleas were encircling her extremities as buzzards would over a dead carcass. Standing a foot-an-a-half off the ground, she was no more than four feet from head to the tip of her scrawny tail. Her diminutive size reminded him of a beagle he once owned back home in Delaware.

Chuck called out to Sal who remained some thirty yards back, "She's downright ugly, man."

"Careful, Chuck. You don't know what she's liable to do," Sal yelled back.

"I will, but I don't think she'll be any trouble," Chuck replied, while crouching down to get a closer look. He noticed that the dog's nose was protracted, even for a canine, and bent slightly to one side. As an elf's, one ear pointed skyward. The other, however, remained semi-erect, personifying a perfect right angle.

Chuck was right. This was the homeliest mongrel he'd ever seen. Yet, for some strange reason, he found himself drawn to her in spite of the animal's physical faults. Perhaps it was the dog's tenacity to survive that provided the common bond. The real reason didn't seem to matter.

Chuck remained crouched while watching the animal burrow through the garbage. It was difficult for him not to feel sorry.

"Sal?"

"What?" he asked.

"Go inside the tent and get me a can of wieners. There should be a few left in the package I got last week from my parents."

"Okay. I'll be right back," Sal said.

"Hurry," Chuck yelled.

In the meantime, Chuck tried to get the dog's attention.

"Hey, girl. Would you like some wieners? I bet you would."

The dog was inattentive. She was more concerned with finding her next meal sniffing around the dump.

Sal returned in less than a minute. "Chuck! Here's the can," he said. "Do you want me to walk it over?"

"No," Chuck replied. "She's skittish. Just toss it to me."

Sal did as requested.

Chuck caught the can with a one-handed stab. Not wasting time, he popped off the lid. Trying again to get the dog's attention, he whistled and called out, "Here, lady, come get some grub." The dog looked at him but an instant before turning back toward the garbage she was rummaging through.

Maybe I should just walk over and dump the can near her, he thought. And that's exactly what he did. Taking a few steps forward, he stopped short, shook the contents of the can onto the ground and backed off. The dog must have sensed the human meant no harm, although she never took her eyes off him while he approached. After Chuck moved away, she walked toward the treats.

"You think she'll eat any?" Sal asked from a distance.

Chuck didn't answer fearing he would scare the dog away.

The aroma was too much for any animal to resist. Taking a final gaze at Chuck, she put her head down and devoured the processed franks in a few voracious bites. Licking her chops several times, she looked up as if to offer thanks. Chuck would later swear he detected a smile on her face.

Chuck moved closer. "Here, Lady," he said.

The name stuck. With head hung low and her tail between her legs, the dog cautiously walked toward him. As Chuck extended his hand to pet the animal, she cowered. Being careful not to startle her, he did everything in slow motion. Bending down to his knees, he placed his hand on her head and slowly petted her, first her head, then all the way back to her tail. The bonding process had commenced. Chuck may not have realized it at the time, but during the process he assumed a responsibility he did not ask for; but, eventually, he knew he had to uphold.

"Sal," Chuck yelled. "Go get me some rope."

"I'll be back in a flash, man."

The nursing and nourishing back to health took weeks. Besides a square meal or two each day, Chuck gave Lady a bath twice a week but only after the animal's utmost reluctance. He also built a dog coop and holding area where she could run.

"Chuck," Sal said.

"What?"

"I don't think your dog likes the pen."

"Why do you say that?"

"Because she's constantly digging holes under the fence."

Chuck knew from the start, although he didn't want to admit it, that Lady would not take kindly to confinement. Listening to Sal's words, Chuck thought it funny and showed it on his face.

"Why are you smirking?" Sal asked.

"It's ironic," said Chuck.

"Okay," Sal said. "I'll bite. Why?"

"She's in a holding pen, and so are we. The only difference is ours is larger. Who's got it worse?"

Sal looked at Chuck, placed his hands on his hips, and said, "I hate it when you get philosophical on me, man."

Chuck smiled and walked back to his tent before turning halfway around to say, "Well, it's true."

Before sunset, Chuck and Sal returned to the pen to do what was agreed upon between the two earlier in the evening. Without fanfare, Lady was liberated. It wasn't like Charles de Gaulle marching through the streets of Paris or Douglas MacArthur's triumphant return to the Philippines during World War II. Chuck Newell merely opened the gate and allowed Lady her freedom.

"Okay, girl. You've been granted a reprieve. I hope she comes back," he told Sal, as he watched Lady bolt from the pen.

Sal patted Chuck on the back and said, "She will."

Lady did come back. Although she took occasional excursions outside the compound, she always returned, if not immediately, usually within twenty-four hours. The abundant food supply and Chuck's unwavering love became the extended leash.

Now that Lady was no longer confined to a pen, she preferred to sleep at the foot of her Master's cot. Late at night, Chuck

My Lady

watched as Lady flattened her bed — a rudimentary mattress Chuck configured out of old towels stuffed into a worn and soiled pillowcase. Stepping onto the pillow, Lady looked around and trampled down the bedding while walking in a circle, over and over.

"Lady! Lie down for God sake. You're making me dizzy," Chuck told her. Within a minute, she was sound asleep.

At the crack of dawn, Lady would wake, walk over to Chuck's cot and lick his face as a subtle reminder to let her out. Her greeting never failed to produce the desired result. Within minutes she was back inside the tent. For the next 20 minutes or so, depending on how lazy Chuck felt that day, she would lie at his side until he rolled out of bed. It wasn't long before both vacated the tent to welcome a new day.

"Hey, Chuck. Is that all she does?" said a fellow soldier who noticed Lady in a compromising position with a dog of the male gender. Procreating became nearly as important to Lady as eating and sleeping. It would be fair to say, Lady was no lady.

Chuck shouted back: "Jealous?"

The soldier laughed, gave a thumbs-up, and continued on his way.

When not romantically inclined, Lady spent a good deal of time with Chuck in the field. It wasn't long before she qualified for an Air Medal; an Animal Air Medal, that is. Getting on a helicopter was easy; knowing when it was safe to disembark was another — anything above six feet and Lady wouldn't budge. If the troops could have grasped the same concept, there would have been far fewer broken limbs. Lady also had an uncanny sense. She followed Chuck like glue, always sniffing and alert to danger with ears persistently listening for sounds in the bush. She was an enormous asset. Just her presence made the men feel much more secure.

One afternoon the platoon made its way to the edge of a clearing. Suddenly, Lady stopped dead in her tracks. She didn't point and she didn't budge, but the hair on the back of her neck stood at attention. Chuck knew something wasn't right.

This is it, baby. There's no turning back. "Hey, Lieutenant," Chuck said, "Look at Lady."

Gazing at the dog, the lieutenant thought his worst fears were about to be realized. Immediately, he issued an order: "Take the safety off, men."

Suddenly, before anyone could react, a pack of wild chickens emerged from behind some elephant grass. Lady had waited long enough. Springing from her position as if launched by a jet engine, she began the chase. For nearly a minute, everyone in the platoon laughed as they watched Lady trying her best to catch, what soon became, an elusive dinner. It didn't take long before Lady ran out of gas. Fortunately for the chickens, they lived to see another day.

October brought the rains. Lady spent much of her time with Chuck and Sal in the tent cowering from the torrential downpours and snarling wind. Miserable was the only way to describe the weather. During the next three months, neither man nor dog saw much action, as conditions proved unsuitable for even the heartiest of creatures, large or small.

When January arrived, all were pleased to shake-off the dampness and for the first time in months, see the sun for longer than a half-hour.

Chuck was cleaning his rifle outside the tent one day when he officially declared himself a thirty-day, short-timer to Sal.

"Hey, Chuck," Sal said. "Congratulations, man. How does it feel?"

"Great . . . indescribable," Chuck said. Suddenly, it dawned on him. "Sal, I'm out of here in a month. I'm gonna' need someone to take care of Lady. There's no way they'll let her come home with me."

"Chuck. I'll take care of her. Don't worry. I've got four months to go."

"I was hoping you'd say that," Chuck said. He not only sounded but also looked relived.

About a week later, Lady departed on one of her many adventures outside the compound. As the evening wore on, Chuck became concerned.

"Where the hell is she?" Chuck said.

Sal replied, "Don't worry man. She's probably chasing chickens. This isn't the first time, and it won't be the last."

"I suppose you're right."

Both men went to sleep. When they awoke in the morning, Lady was nowhere to be found.

"Sal."

"What?" Sal asked.

"I've got a bad feeling about Lady."

"Take it easy," Sal said. "It's only been a day."

Days passed then an entire week elapsed. Chuck posted notices all over the compound advertising a twenty-five dollar reward for Lady's safe return. He left flyers in the mess, near the mailroom, even the latrine.

Lady's fate was finally revealed when a platoon came across her remains near the side of a trail, outside the local village. She had been dead for several days, confirmed by the body's advanced state of decomposition. The evidence was conclusive. Lady had been shot. Sal broke the news to Chuck early that evening.

"Rumors suggest one of our own men did her in."

"No," Chuck said, not wanting to believe his ears.

"I'm sorry to say, it's true," Sal said. "Someone decided to use her for target practice." Sal pulled no punches in conveying the message. "As I heard it, a bullet hit her behind the left ear exiting through her neck. Another round hit her in the shoulder. The first wound, whichever one, proved fatal." Looking at Chuck, Sal continued. "She never knew what hit her;" then he added, "I'm sorry I had to be the messenger."

Chuck turned to wipe a tear from his eye. Then, he became angry, as he looked at Sal and said, "What kind of a person would do such a thing?"

"One hell of a son-of-a-bitch," Sal responded.

Early the following morning, Chuck rolled from his cot. He hardly slept during the night.

"Sal, wake up!"

"What?"

"Wake up," Chuck repeated.

"What time is it?"

95

"Four-thirty."

"Four-thirty? Why are ya getting' me up so early?"

"We've got a job to do," Chuck said. "We're gonna find Lady's remains and give her a proper burial."

"Can't we wait an hour?" Sal asked, pulling the sheet over his head.

"No, we can't. In a couple of hours it'll be full daylight. It won't be safe for the two of us to be walking around out there."

"Damn! All right. Give me some time to get my fatigues on."

While Sal dressed, Chuck picked up a piece of wood he had fashioned into a small rudimentary cross. It came from the slates of a discarded pallet he found the night before near the PX. Working into the early hours of the morning, using his jackknife, he carved out an epitaph on the horizontal slat of the cross and placed it in his rucksack, along with an entrenching tool and a regulation U.S. Army poncho.

"You ready yet?" Chuck said.

"Give me a minute to tie my boots, God damn it!"

After a trek of less than 30 minutes, they located what was left of Lady's earthly remains, exactly where Sal had been told they could be found. Chuck wrapped what was left of her body in the poncho he brought.

"Where should we bury her?" Sal asked, nervous to be out on an open trail away from the safe confines of the compound.

Chuck looked around and saw a large rock near a scattering of small eucalyptus just off the trail. "Over there," he said.

"I'll dig the hole, Chuck." Sal took the entrenching tool and had the hole dug in a couple of minutes.

When Sal finished, Chuck gently placed Lady's remains at the bottom, took the shovel from Sal's hands and covered them until no loose dirt remained. Tears welled in his eyes as he recited a brief prayer — perhaps there is no heaven for animals, but it made him feel better. Finding a rock slightly larger than his palm, Chuck banged the cross into the ground.

Chuck Newell made it back to "the World." Amazingly, even after all the years, he couldn't forget Lady and all the fun and love she provided. Occasionally, he prayed for the soul of that unknown American soldier who though it sport to snuff out the life of one of God's harmless creations. Chuck thought it odd. In many ways, the unknown soldier, too, was a victim of that terrible war.

Outside the village of Thuy Hoa, there may still exist, although it's highly doubtful, a small, weather-beaten cross on the side of what today may be an obscure and overgrown trail. The message Chuck etched has long since been obliterated by the elements. Yet, Chuck will never forget his heartfelt sentiment:

HERE LIES MY LADY
A VICTIM OF THE ENEMY

THE CONFESSION

The confession of one man humbles all.
-Antonio Porschia, *Voices* (1968).

"**N**urses! Please gather 'round. Stand a little closer, thank you. I don't want to shout. Welcome to the fifth floor. My name is Abby, Abby Fiedler. I'm your shift supervisor. You may have heard of me. If you have, whether you believe my reputation is the least of my concerns. Perhaps, I am distant and cold. Understand that my primary responsibility is to the patients and staff of this hospital. Thus, it is my duty to assure you perform all of your assignments with dignity and in a professional manner."

She continued: "I have a few items to discuss before you start your rounds. On this floor, you'll be busier than you could ever imagine. Before long, you'll learn there's not enough time during your shift to do everything that needs to be done. Unfortunately there's nothing that can be done to remedy the situation. Between finding good nurses and budget constraints, we have learned to make do. So will you. My advice is simple: waste as little time and energy as possible. Although this may sound a bit harsh, you've got to learn to dissociate yourself from your patients." She hesitated a second before continuing. "Now, I'm not saying, don't be a good nurse. However, please appreciate that there's a fine line between providing quality medical care and becoming too attached to the patient. Also remember, you'll be dealing with terminal cases, day in and day out, throughout the entire time you work here. If you refuse to heed my warning, you'll become useless. When that happens, you will be reassigned to another ward. Remember, never let yourself become emotionally involved with any of your patients."

Marie transferred to the terminally ill ward over a year ago. She served as a registered nurse for over nineteen years, the last twelve as staff at New York's Veterans Hospital. Marie loved her profession in spite of how insidious and tumultuous it could be. The nursing care she provided was always difficult; yet, to her, the personal rewards far outweighed the low pay and long hours. Over the past year, Marie had come to see it all: major traumas, alcohol poisoning, drug overdoses, comatose patients, cancer victims, and AIDS sufferers.

Somehow, within the last few months, she and Abby became close friends. Marie always acted as a professional, and that is what bonded the two women. In return, Abby treated Marie with the same courtesy.

Abby and Marie came from the same densely populated area of Long Island, a predominately Italian neighborhood. Because of their slight difference in age, they never went to school together although they did graduate from the same high school. Neither was Italian. But, like most folks, they thoroughly enjoyed the cuisine, perhaps a little too much. Both were overweight.

Abby had been divorced for several years and had two grown children. Neither lived at home. Marie never married but it wasn't because she didn't have opportunities. She met some wonderful guys, even fell in love a few times, but things never worked out. Perhaps, she was to blame. Her career always seemed to take precedence.

One afternoon late in the shift, Abby and Marie were on coffee break chitchatting about what else: food.

"Marie, when was the last time you ate at Tony's Restaurant on the shore?"

"Tony's! My God, I bet it's been a good 20 years. What made you think of that place?"

"At lunch, one of the young nurses was heating leftover lasagna in the microwave. The smell made me think of Tony's. Mmmm . . . they had the best lasagna I've ever tasted in my entire life. They used four different cheeses and a rich, sweet homemade tomato sauce. The hamburger meat was freshly ground with loads and loads of garlic. I bet the lasagna was four inches thick."

"Stop it! You're making me hungry," Marie laughed. "You know, my parents used to take my little brother and me there all the time. And you're right. The lasagna was out of this world. I'd love to go back."

"Why don't we?"

"What do you mean?"

"Tomorrow after work, why don't we take the train out to the Island? We'll be there by six. We can enjoy cocktails and a leisurely meal and be back to our homes no later than nine. That is if you don't have plans for the evening."

"What plans? All I have to do is pick up a few groceries. I can do that any time. You know, I'd love to go there again."

"Are we on for tomorrow night then?"

"Why not?" Marie responded. "By all means."

"Terrific. I'll meet you downstairs in the main lobby around five," Abby said, as she pulled a chart off the wall and walked out the door to check on the nurses making their rounds throughout the ward.

Marie continued to sit at the table thinking about the reasons why the others misunderstood her friend. Abby wasn't anywhere near as thick-skinned as many thought, at least not to Marie. Abby had an image to uphold, and an image meant everything in her profession. *Perhaps the rumors about her are true,* Marie though. *She rarely smiled and was overly demanding.* Then she rationalized, *but she was always knowledgeable and fair.*

The 5:30 p.m. train leading toward the Island was always late. Today, both ladies were lucky. The delay was only several minutes. Abby and Marie boarded the train a few blocks from work and rode the line for 35 minutes, stopping several times along the way to pick up passengers. Few disembarked. Abby and Marie made some small talk, but each wanted to sit back and relax. Their day was especially trying. Three patients succumbed on their floor during the afternoon. The deaths were all expected but each time a patient dies it takes something out of a nurse. Death is death, even to a nurse working in a terminally ill ward.

Just as Marie slipped her shoes off, the train came to a stop. Quickly, Marie slipped them on. The ladies disembarked. Taxis were abundant and Abby hailed a cab. "Tony's please," she said to the driver. In a matter of minutes they arrived in front of the eating establishment.

"That'll be eight bucks, ma'am," the driver said.

Marie fumbled for her wallet in her pocketbook. Abby beat her to the punch.

"I got it," Abby insisted. Still looking at Marie, she said, "Marie, you can pay on the way back." Handing the bill to the driver Abby said, "Here's ten, keep the change." The ladies opened the door closest to the sidewalk and stepped out.

"Thanks, ma'am. Have a good evening," the driver stated as he sped off.

"Hasn't changed much, has it?" Abby asked. Abby and Marie were standing outside the restaurant near a full parking lot looking at the same building façade they remembered as kids. Tony's Restaurant was printed in large black letters above the main door. Beneath, written in small script letters, was the restaurant's advertising slogan: *The Best Italian Eatery on the Island.*

"Looks the same to me. I hope the food hasn't changed. Come on. Let's go in," Abby said.

Meeting them at the second door was a comely young hostess. "Ladies, do you have reservations?" she asked.

Dumbfounded, Abby and Marie looked at each other. Neither thought to make any. "No, we haven't," Abby said. "How long is the wait?"

"About an hour to an hour and ten minutes."

Abby and Marie knew they were committed: so what if their schedule was delayed an hour? Abby spoke first. "Are there vacant seats in the lounge?"

"I just came from upstairs and there are a few empty tables," said the hostess. "May I have your name please?"

"Ferguson," Marie said.

Abby and Marie walked up the short flight of stairs and quickly made their way to an empty table in the corner of the room. After some idle chatter, a waiter came over to take their drink order.

"Could I have a glass of Zinfandel?" Marie inquired.

"White or red?" the waiter asked.

"White, if you please."

"House okay, ma'am?"

"That'll be fine," Marie said.

Abby thought for a while before placing her order. "I'd like a Cabernet Sauvignon," she said.

"Tonight we're featuring a fine Belgian wine. It's robust, with a pleasant bouquet and just a hint of plums and black cherry. Reasonably priced, I may add. May I entice you with a glass, madam?"

"Sounds lovely. Yes, you may."

"Thank you, ladies. I'll be back shortly with your wine. In the meantime, please help yourself to the cheese and crackers," he said as he pointed to a small table near the bar.

"Shall we?" Abby asked.

After filling their plates with chunks of cheese and thin wheat crackers, they returned to their seats. A minute later, the waiter returned with their drinks.

"Enjoy your wine, ladies. If I can be of any further service, please call me. My name is Peter."

Abby said thanks. Marie followed suit.

Abby was first to raise her glass to toast the evening. "Here's to delightful company, a wonderful meal and . . . a brief escape from our profession."

"Here, here!" Marie said.

After more small talk, both ladies were running out of things to say.

Never much of a conversationalist, Marie began to feel awkward as she could only talk about food and the weather for so long. Abby and Marie had just become friends and, to this point, work was their only common bond. *Why not steer the conversation toward work?* Marie asked herself.

"Abby."

"Yes, Marie."

"If I'm being too presumptuous please let me know, but I always wondered about the first instructions you gave us."

"What do you mean?"

"You know, when you told us not to get emotionally involved with the patients. It's not the first time I've heard such a speech. Yours, however, seemed to have hidden meaning."

"Marie . . . you're very perceptive. I don't know if I'd go as far to call it that. Perhaps a better explanation would be . . . lessons learned." Abby paused a second to take another sip of her Cabernet and a bite of cracker and cheese. "You know, Marie. When I started on this floor, I was given similar instructions. I thought I knew everything there ever was to know about rendering quality nursing care and good bedside manners. It wasn't long before I found out otherwise."

Abby became introspective. Marie had never seen Abby this way and wondered if her own line of questioning was inappropriate. Marie looked at her and said, "Perhaps we should talk about something else," not knowing what that something else should be.

"No. I'm glad you brought it up," Abby said. "I never talked to anyone about this before, and maybe now is as good a time as any. That is, if you care to listen."

"Why sure," Marie said. Usually it was the other way around. Marie, and all the other nurses, always asked Abby for an opinion about a particular case or procedure. They also requested advice about issues unrelated to their profession, such as their personal lives. After all, Abby was their supervisor. Aren't supervisors supposed to serve as counselors to their subordinates? Problems rolled off them like water off a duck's back.

"Marie, our jobs — yours and mine — are extremely difficult; sometimes they're damn near impossible. Our equipment and facilities are antiquated. Topping it all off, we're incredibly overworked — doctors, nurses and the staff. Having to face the grim reaper each and every day has to take a toll. Take today. How many did we lose?"

Marie guessed: "Three," she said.

"Marie. I don't even know. Isn't that sad?" She looked a bit perplexed." "I've been at this for so long, I never keep count anymore. What purpose would it serve?"

A Night of Wine, Dinner, and Candid Conversation

Abby had never talked about losing patients before, at least not to me. I wouldn't say hearing her talk this way was a shock, but it was an eye-opener. Perhaps the wine was loosening her lips.

"If you let yourself get too close, it'll tear you apart. I tried to remain aloof." Abby took another sip of wine and slowly set it down on the table. She had already consumed more than half a glass in a short time. Twisting the glass with her fingers as it rested on the table, she continued. "Before becoming a shift supervisor, I had to earn my wings just as you're doing now. Everything seemed to be progressing just fine. I was pleased with myself and thought I was in control, especially with my inner self. There was no question in my mind that I had become insulated to all the pain and suffering. Before starting my shift each day, I reminded myself not to get too close with any of my wards. Then one day, my glass house slowly came crashing down."

"What happened?" Marie asked.

"Just before Thanksgiving, back in 1995 . . . no, I'm sorry, it was '96 — I remember it was an election year — a patient named Gabriel Vaillencourt was brought to my ward in a wheelchair. There wasn't much they could do for him downstairs. The advanced stages of AIDS were starting to ravage his already, frail body. He had these nasty sores all over. I've seen sores before on AIDS patients, but his were disgusting and seemed to grow larger by the day. All we could do was make him comfortable, an amazing feat when you consider the seriousness of the disease. Most of the time, he was on painkillers. Yet, all things considered, his mind was sharp. How he managed to remain coherent, with all the pain and medication, is beyond my wildest imagination, yet he did. What a trooper. The poor man rarely complained or asked for special attention."

"That's a switch," Marie said. Then she realized the potential impact of her words. "Abby, I didn't mean to sound like they're all problems. Sometimes, a rotten apple makes you forget about all the decent patients."

"I understand," Abby said. She took another sip of wine, just as Peter, our waiter, returned.

"Ladies, may I bring you another wine? I just checked with the hostess and you've got at least another forty minutes before you'll be seated."

"Marie?"

"Sure," Marie said.

"The same wine, ladies?"

Abby and Marie nodded their heads.

After Peter walked away, Marie said to Abby, "Please go on."

Abby clasped her hands around the wine glass as she continued to tell the final installment of her story.

"Gabriel reminded me, at least in looks, of a man I once knew while attending college. There was never a love affair, at least not a full-blown one, between David and me, but we liked each other's company a great deal. When we graduated, he went his way — Madison Avenue — and I went into nursing. I never saw him again," as she slowly bowed her head down toward the wine glass. Avoiding eye contact, she continued. "I always wondered if there could have been more between us." Finally looking up as if relieved at what she told Marie, she said "Oh well, it's too late now, I suppose!" as she lifted the glass of wine to her lips and sipped.

Marie wanted to learn more. "So what happened?"

"Gabriel — Gabe we called him — hadn't been on my floor for more than a few days when I decided to look into his records. Call it feminine curiosity. Maybe it was because he reminded me so much of David. Perhaps it was both. That night I spent a good half-hour looking through his medical file. The folder was unusually thick. I noticed that he served in the infantry in Vietnam starting in 1967. He was wounded in the shoulder by shrapnel, but the wound was superficial. Within days, he returned to duty. Late in 1968, Gabe was granted an Honorable Discharge, but I noticed that his visits to VA hospitals commenced only a few months later."

"Was it mental or physical?" Marie asked.

"Both, but his predominant problem was mental. Not long after he returned from Vietnam, he was treated for depression. There were also annotations that he received counseling for combat fatigue, but it was on an irregular basis. There were VA hospitals from here to Florida and as far away as California listed in the documents. If I had to guess, I'd say he wandered the country not staying long in any particular location. You know what else?"

"No, what," Marie asked?

"He had a serious drug addiction — heroin first, later cocaine. I found at least two incidents of accidental overdose."

"Probably that's how he contracted AIDS," Marie replied.

"That'd be my guess. Living on the streets and all, hypodermic needles were passed around like cigarettes. What a shame."

"That's for sure. So what happened after you read his file?" Marie persisted being more inquisitive than ever before.

"It's strange. I mean, I . . . well . . . I felt bad for him. That was my initial mistake, you know, having feelings. Slowly, I lost my objectivity as a nurse. Each day, I spent a little more time at his bedside, not that I was overlooking my other patients. It was just that he was . . . well, special. At first we talked for only a few minutes each day. After the first week, I was spending ten to fifteen minutes with him at least three to four times a day. My supervisor, who long since retired, never caught on. For that matter, even I was clueless. At the time, it never dawned on me that I was engaged in something unprofessional. I mean I made a huge mistake. I let myself become emotionally attached to a patient."

"How long did he suffer?"

"Not long, thank God. He never made it 'til Christmas. During the final days, he couldn't move or talk. On the 22nd, he lapsed into a coma. Although his death troubled me, what he confessed a few weeks previous bothered me more."

"And what was that?" Marie asked, as all kinds of scenarios played out in her mind.

Abby let out a long breath of air before continuing. "Something was eating at him, and it wasn't about dying. I think he prepared himself for that fairly well." She took another sip of wine. "I could tell . . . I could feel it in my bones. That's when I made a cardinal mistake. A week or so before he died, I asked him, point blank, what was wrong."

Marie had been in the nursing profession long enough to know what Abby was feeling. She tried to comfort her the best she could.

"Abby, we've all made similar mistakes. We're only human. Well . . . we are you know."

"Thank you, Marie," she said. "But the situation I placed myself in became even more difficult."

"What do you mean?" Marie asked.

Abby sighed before responding. "Early one evening, I sat on the side of his bed and without pulling any punches I asked him what was bothering him. As I did so, I brushed his hair back from his eyes. Without thinking, I was breaking yet another cardinal sin of nursing: 'Thou shall not get too physical with a patient.'"

"Abby. You were being compassionate, nothing more."

"I suppose. But I'm a nurse. My actions shouldn't be laced with emotion."

"See it as you will, but I don't think you did anything out of the ordinary. So, what did he say?"

"He didn't answer, at least not immediately. He just looked away and stared out the window. Then he mumbled some words. I asked him to repeat them. He turned toward me and spoke louder, but soft enough not to be heard by the other patients in the room.

"'I think I killed somebody.'"

"'What,' I said, hardly believing my ears."

"'I think I killed somebody . . . in 'Nam.'"

"The pain on his face was heavy, and his torment tore at my soul. Today, I'm unsure if Gabe suffered more from the secret he held inside all those years or the effects of that terrible disease."

"I tried to comfort him the best I could when I said, 'That's understandable, Gabe. After all, you fought in a war.'"

"'Listen,' he said, as he grabbed my arm. 'You don't understand.'"

"'What don't I understand, Gabe?' I replied."

"'He was one of ours.'"

"'What do you mean, *one of ours*?' I asked. Marie, I've got to be honest. I was dumbfounded. I guess I didn't want to believe what I'd just heard. Then he elaborated."

"'He was our platoon's second lieutenant.'"

"I didn't know what to say. The shock of hearing such a thing was overwhelming. For the first time, it dawned on me that I had gotten myself into a situation I should never have. When my brain thawed, the first question that came to mind was, 'Do you want to speak to a priest or minister?'"

"'Please, no,' he said."

"Oh, my! Did he tell you anything else?" Marie asked.

"Yes. I sat and listened to the entire story. What else could I do, Marie? After all, I'd already dug the hole."

"It must have been hard."

"It was . . . very difficult; more than anyone could ever imagine."

"Why did he do such a thing?" Marie asked.

"He wasn't sure that his bullet killed the lieutenant. He said it could have been any member of his platoon, perhaps all of them. I remember his words were slurred, and it was painful for him to speak. I can't remember his exact words, but I think it went something like this:

'A new second lieutenant was assigned to our unit shortly after a sniper killed our first lieutenant. The guy was gung-ho from the start and had no idea what 'Nam was about. After several patrols in which he nearly got us all killed because of
his over-aggressiveness and stupidity, we decided to waste him. There didn't seem to be any other way. It was either his life or ours. We decided to take care of business in the field. It didn't take long. It wasn't a week later when we were walking up a path, and all hell broke loose. The second lieutenant was walking point. The first rounds shot by us were all in his direction. He went down like a pile of bricks. I don't know if my bullet hit him or not. Maybe all the rounds did. All I know is, from that second on, no one ever spoke about it again. After the firefight, his body was placed in a helicopter and sent to a field mortuary. Five days later the remains were flown back to the States. He was buried a hero, and we were still alive.'"

Abby reminisced: "I imagine Gabe spent his entire life trying to hide, most likely from himself, never able to bury his guilt. When I left his bed that afternoon, all I could say was, 'Gabe, I believe God understands.' For the first time since he arrived, I detected a slight smile upon his face. Whether I believed what I was saying wasn't relative. That he believed what I said was far more important. From that single incident, I learned my lesson and learned it well."

"Abby," Marie said. "I had no idea. That must have been extremely painful." But before Marie could say another word, the waiter returned.

"Ladies, we have a splendid table set for you near the fireplace. Kindly follow me, please."

Tony's Restaurant hadn't changed much over the years, either the decor or the cuisine. The meal was everything Abby and Marie envisioned, and then some. But for Marie, the evening was an eye-opener. After nearly twenty years of nursing, she finally understood the realities of her profession: that nurses aren't perfectionists; seriously ill patients almost always suffer, sometimes with and sometimes without a viable explanation, and eventually most die. What Abby perceived as her own character flaw, Marie accepted as an enviable trait. A nurse's primary duty is to comfort her patients, as difficult as it may be, especially when there are no guarantees of tomorrows.

Gabe's Confession

THE CHRISTMAS TREE

I'm dreaming of a white Christmas, just like the ones I use to know.
-Irving Berlin, *White Christmas*, (1942)

*D*ear Ma and Pa,
How is everything back home? Everything is fine here. How was your Thanksgiving? Did everyone get enough to eat? Mom with your cooking I bet they did. Did Pa and Jimmy eat the legs like they usually do? Who won the wishbone pulling contest?

Tell Jimmy and Nancy that I picked them up a soovaneer. I think they will like it some. I got them in Da Nang. I'll bring them when I come home.

Don't worry about me. As I told you before I'm in a safe place. Nothing much happens here althouh I do have a funny story to tell you. A few days ago we got rid of some local Vietnamese who filled sandbags for us. We paid them about two cents a bag. We didn't need no more sandbags so the major told them to go home and not come back. Guess what? That night we took 5 rounds of mortars from the village. Who do you think fired them? Ha! No one got hurt. I learned a long time ago never to trust these people.

Tell Nancy I got her card and what was inside it. It is realy cute. She's getting real smart for 8 years old. Tell her I like her school picture lots and I put it in my wallet.

The last letter that I got from you guys was dated 2 weeks ago. Usualy it gets here in about 8 days.

You asked if I needed any thing. Is there any way you could send me a small fake Xmas tree? Me and Brad were talking about deccorating one and putting it in the corner of our tent. It has got to be a small one or the post office won't let you mail it. By the way did it snow yet?

Bob Hope is in Da Nang filming his Xmas show. They won't let any of us go. Colonel Burnham says he needs every one of us here and not there. He is always putting us on red alert. Nothing

112

ever happens. I think he is scared that if something happens and he doesn't have us around he will be blamed for it and lose rank.

We heard some talk about a peace conforance with North Vietnam. Anything to it? I hope so. We are always hearing things about peace talks but nothing ever comes of it. This war is really stupid. Ha!

I'm now officialy a short-timer. Only 90 more days to go. Don't rent out my room because I'm going to be home before you can say North Carolina. Ha!

Miss you guys.

Love,

Justin

PS: Please tell Andrea that I miss her a ton. When I get a chance I will write her a letter but don't have much time now. I only have time for this short note. So please tell her that I will write her soon.

"Justin. What's in the package?"

"I think it's the Christmas tree I asked fer from my Ma and Pa."

"Well, aren't you gonna open it?" asked Brad.

"What fer? I gotta pull guard duty tonight. If I take it out of the box, someone's probably gonna steal it. I'll jes leave it right cher by my bunk an' cover it with a blanket. We can open it tomorrow. You don't have guard tomorrow, do ya?"

"Nope."

"Good. We'll open it after supper."

"Justin?"

"What?"

"What are we gonna hang on the tree? We ain't got no ornaments."

"Don't fret none. I gave that a lot of thinkin'. I've got it all figured out here in my little brain," Justin said with confidence. "We're gonna have the best doggone Christmas tree this side of the Mekong Delta. Trust me, little fella'."

"Sounds great, Justin. I can't wait. Anything to get my mind outta this place."

Justin and Brad walked the short distance to their tent after eating supper at the makeshift mess hall. This evening they had two meal choices: hamburgers with canned green beans and imitation mashed potatoes or hamburgers with canned green beans, imitation mashed potatoes and gravy — a subtle change from the previous evening's provisions. As always, the men were given the option of having their hamburgers cooked to order. Justin wanted his medium, the same way he always devoured his meat. Brad decided to change from medium to well done. Yesterday, when he ordered his burger, it came out mooing. Tonight, much to his chagrin, it was served well done.

"Brad. When I get back to the World, I ain't gonna eat anotha' hamburger fer months."

"Ya tellin' me. Mine was worse than leather," said Brad, as he spit on the ground in disgust. "Ya know what amazes me?"

"What's that?"

"I've been eatin' this stuff for all this time and I ain't got sick yet."

"Fer sure," Justin responded. "But ya know, we've been poisoned anyway."

"Whatta you mean?"

Justin snickered. "All the saltpeter they've been puttin' in our mashed potatoes has killed our sex drive. It's gonna take months before we get it back."

"Maybe you," Brad said, "but not me, big guy!"

Brad and Justin laughed heartily as they walked into the tent.

Justin sat on his cot as Brad spread out on his. Brad spoke first.

"Hey! Ain't we gonna open the box from your folks?"

"Ya darn right we are."

Justin got up from his cot, picked up the cardboard box, and placed it directly in front of him on the cot. Brad bounced up in an instant and stood next to his buddy. Opening packages from home or watching someone doing the honor was always fun. Justin briefly gazed at the delivery address:

To: PFC Justin E. Harrington
US 79727384
Co. C., 3rd Battalion, 21st Infantry
1st Infantry Division
APO San Francisco, California 96225

Next, he looked at the postmark. The mailing date was barely legible in smeared black ink near the canceled postage stamps on the upper right hand corner of the box. The package was shipped from Bakersville, North Carolina, two weeks previous. The date was the 17th of December. Wrapped in brown paper, it was sealed in several places with wide strips of cellophane tape. Stamped on the lower left in red, one-inch letters was the word: FRAGILE.

"Brad. Let me borrow ya knife."

"Here you go," Brad said, as he handed his jackknife to Justin.

Quickly, Justin cut through the tape and tore off the paper. He was now staring at a cardboard box that was tightly sealed with more strands of cellophane shipping tape. At one end, on top of the package, he stabbed the jackknife into the cardboard box and pulled it slowly toward him, cutting the tape along the way. Immediately, they detected the unmistakable scent of spruce. The smell was wonderful, something neither of them expected. Justin excitedly cut the corners on each side and opened the flaps.

"What the heck!" Justin exclaimed as he peered into the box.

Brad stared, dumbfounded.

Inside the cardboard box was a Christmas tree all right. Only this Christmas tree wasn't an imitation. It was the real McCoy. There was only a slight, insurmountable problem. Sticking his hand in, Justin pulled out a small, two-foot tree as he held it in front of him.

"What the hell is this?" he asked. In his hand he held a poor example of what once could have been a perfectly good miniature Christmas tree. Barely a needle clung to the limbs. The rest had fallen off, browned and scattered on the bottom of the box. The high heat and humidity had taken its dreadful toll, perhaps as early as several days ago.

Justin peered at Brad and said with a quizzical look, "I could swear I told 'em to send me an imitation tree."

115

Brad laughed and said, "The thing looks more like a bottle brush than a Christmas tree."

Justin laughed at Brad's comparison.

At the bottom of the box, strewn with all the fallen needles was a small white envelope. Justin ripped open the sealed envelope with his fingers and pulled out a note. He read it aloud:

Dear Justin,

Pa wanted you to have a real tree. He went out this morning and cut one down from the field near the east pasture. He said it wouldn't be right to have a fake one after having a real one for all these years. Pa made a small wooden stand in the barn and nailed it on, figuring to save you some time.

Like me, he's worried sick about you, but he won't let it out . .

Justin stopped reading aloud as it became apparent the note was becoming too personal. He read the rest in silence:

. . . That's the way he is. He loves you and wants you to come home, but he finds it hard to put it into words.

We were running short of time and wanted you to get the tree before Christmas, so Pa wrapped it and dropped it off at the post office this afternoon.

Merry Christmas, my son, and may God watch over you and bring you and all the other young men safely back home.

I promise to write a longer letter tomorrow.

Love,

Mama

Justin turned slightly to hide his face. He wiped a tear from his eye. Looking back, he sucked in his breath and said, "Whatta we waitin' for, Brad? Let's decorate our Christmas tree, needles or no needles."

"Justin! Decorate it with what?"

"Do I have to do all the thinkin'? Here. Take your jackknife. Grab a pencil an' draw a five-pointed star on the cardboard box, unless you're good at drawin' angels," he chuckled.

"How big do I make it?"

"No bigger than four to five inches."

Brad did as told. Moments later, he asked, "Now what do I do?"

"Cut it out with your jackknife," Brad instructed.

A bit perplexed about his task, Brad played along. Using the jackknife as a saw and the pencil lines as a guide, he cut through the cardboard with the precision of a fine craftsman.

"How's this?" as he held it up for Justin to see.

"Looks great, Brad."

Reminiscent of a magician pulling a rabbit out of a hat, Justin, reached into one of his fatigue pockets, and pulled out a folded sheet of aluminum foil.

"Where'd ya get that?"

"I fetched it from the mess. It was coverin' the mashed potatoes." Wiping the sticky residue from the foil onto his pant leg, he handed it to Brad. "Here, take it," he said.

Brad grabbed the foil and stared at it quizzically. "Now, what do you want me to do with this?" he asked.

With a gleam in his eye, Justin said, "Wrap it 'round the star. That'll be fer the top."

"But what about ornaments? We ain't got any, Justin."

Pointing to the open floor locker next to his cot, he said, "See those pipe cleaners I use to clean my weapon?"

"Ya."

"That's gonna be our candy cane. All ya have to do is bend them over 'bout a third of the way down. They'll be a perfect size fer our tree. As fer garland, remember the care package I got last week from my Aunt Lily?"

"Ya."

"Well, Aunt Lily mailed me cookies all right, but she also sent a paper bag full of gumdrops. I saved them fer our tree."

"What are we gonna do with them?" Brad asked. "If the needles hadn't of fell off, we could have just stuck them on the branches."

"No problem. Get out your sewin' kit like I'm gonna do. String a needle with a long thread. Stick the needle through the gumdrops until you've used them all up. We'll wrap that 'round the tree."

"And what else are we gonna put on it?"

117

"What dah ya think I am, some kind of miracle worker? Let me think a second." Suddenly, he was inspired. "Brad. Look at your fatigues. Do ya notice anythin'?"

"Nah. What the heck am I suppose to see?"

"All the grenade safety pins we saved. Between us there must be at least ten of them thar rings. We can slide 'em over the branches. They'll look great."

"No! Not my grenade pins," pleaded Brad. (Grenade safety pins were a status symbol and served as indisputable evidence that the bearer threw a live grenade in combat.)

"Listen, Brad. It's Christmas time. In a couple of days, you can take 'em back. You won't even miss 'em."

"Can't we use somethin' else?"

"And whatta you suggest we use instead?"

Brad hadn't a clue although, he tried hard to think of something, anything that would not separate him from his conceded possessions. "Oh . . . all right," he conceded, looking the least bit happy.

For the remainder of the evening, both men sat on their cots stringing gumdrops. After completing the makeshift garland and wrapping it around the tree, Justin and Brad stood back and admired their creation, a work of art, at least by their standards.

"Justin."

"What?" Justin replied.

"Do ya want me to get rid of the box?"

"Nope. Not until I dump out the needles. I'll put 'em in somethin' and place 'em under the tree. I reckon we'll be able to smell 'em for at least a few more days."

"Good idea," Brad replied.

During the remainder of their tour, Justin and Brad never forgot the moment. For Justin, however, it meant much more, greater than mere words could say. There was love in that scraggly Christmas tree that only he understood: the love of a father to his beloved son that thousands of miles of separation and a war could never take away.

A few days before departing Vietnam, Justin's father died, a victim of a massive coronary. Justin didn't get the word until he arrived at Ft. Lewis, Washington, for final out-processing. The news came as a shocking blow.

"Pa?" Billy asked. "Isn't it my turn to pick out the tree?"

"It sure is, Billy," Justin replied.

The year was 1987. Billy and his twin brother, Richie, had just turned 13. Ever since they were toddlers, the twins alternated selecting a Christmas tree.

Justin's mother passed away in 1976. Nancy, his sister and only kin, shared in the estate: a modest three-story, colonial farmhouse, a ramshackle barn, and over sixty acres of fertile farmland. But, farming was never in Justin's blood: too strenuous a profession; little time for enjoyment, and only marginal revenue to support a young family.

Not long after returning from the war, Justin found his calling. After working several years as an apprentice, he became a master cabinetmaker. His trade paid good money, especially for someone lacking a college education. As for Nancy, she, too, wanted nothing to do with the farm. In late 1981, Justin and Nancy sold the property to a middle-aged couple from Durham. At the closing, besides the money, Justin insisted on one condition of sale: that during the holiday season, he and his family would be allowed to visit the property and cut down a tree for Christmas. The buyers agreed, and the closing was consummated.

On the fifth of December during the same year, Justin, his wife Ann, and their two boys drove out to the farm. The trip took a little over an hour. Passing the farmhouse, Justin drove another half mile before turning right onto a dirt road that led to a wooded field near a pasture, the same field he played in as a boy.

Pulling the car over to the side of the road and coasting to a stop, Justin shut off the engine. "Okay. Everybody out," he commanded.

Before the boys could make a beeline to the trees, Ann issued a tempered warning: "Remember, Richie, this year it's Billy's turn to pick out the tree."

"I know, Mama," Richie replied.

119

The boys hadn't been in the woods for more than a minute when Billy started yelling. "Pa! Pa! Look at this one. Isn't this one neat?"

Justin trotted over. "Boy. It sure is, Billy!" patting his son on the back.

The tree Billy selected stood a mere five feet high. Sparse and misshapen, it appeared to be the runt of the litter; stunted and overshadowed by all the other spruces two to three times it's height. No one except members of the Harrington family from Bakersville, North Carolina, would have made a similar choice.

Using a bow saw he brought from home, Justin was given the honor of cutting it down. After felling the tree, Billy and Richie dragged it from the woods and slid it onto the back of the station wagon. Closing the tailgate flush against the limbs, Justin secured the tree with twine to the back bumper. "Let's go," he said. All four Harrington's jumped into the car and road off. As Justin neared the farmhouse, not a word was spoken. Justin gave it one last look as his mind began to wander. *All those wonderful years*, he thought. Knowing he wouldn't see the place for another year, his eyes began to water, but not for long. Richie broke the silence.

"Pa?"

"What, Richie?" Justin asked.

"Can you tell us the story again about the Christmas tree your Daddy sent you when you were in Vietnam?"

"Sure can," Justin replied.

It didn't matter how many times they heard the story. To the twins, it always seemed fresh and exhilarating. Even his wife, Ann, listened intently.

"A few days after arrivin' home, I attended my Daddy's funeral," he said. "While kneelin' in church between my Ma and your Aunt Nancy, I made a silent pact. I promised myself that when I had a family, I'd always celebrate the holiday season by havin' a Christmas tree just like the one my Pa gave me. At the time, it seemed like the best way to honor his memory. Besides, I never wanted to forget my Daddy, and havin' a Christmas tree like I had in Vietnam would always remind me of him." Justin gazed in the rearview mirror at his boys before he continued. "I want you to know, I learned somethin' important that day: that it's not about havin' the biggest, the fanciest, or the best; instead, it's learnin' to appreciate the little things, those we always seem to take for granted." He hesitated for a second before continuing. "Boys. Anyone can buy a perfectly trimmed Christmas tree. But how many will remember what it looked like a few days after Christmas? Heck, every Christmas looks the same to those folks. Their Christmases all seem to roll together. Now ours . . well, they're a little special, and the tree we pick each year helps make it that way."

Looking, again, into the rearview mirror, he said with resolve, "Remember, boys. Appearances are deceivin'. It's not always about what you see. Sometimes, it's what you don't see that really matters."

The Christmas Tree

THE ONE QUESTION
NEVER TO ASK A COMBAT VETERAN

What's done is done.
-Shakespeare, *Macbeth*, III, ii

The phone rang. Professor Grainger picked up the receiver.

"Nellie. Your party is waiting," said the receptionist at the other end of the line.

"Thank you, Jean. I'll be right down." Hanging up the phone, she looked at her students and said, "I've got to go downstairs to pick up a guest speaker for my next class. We only have five minutes to go so let's call it a day. Don't forget, there's a quiz next Tuesday."

Several students groaned as they left the classroom.

As the last student departed, Professor Grainger walked out the door, down the stairwell, and after taking an immediate right, found herself in front of the Dean's office. Her guest speaker was standing inside talking to the secretary. She looked at him from outside the door before entering. He appeared to be about six feet tall, on the lanky side, with long brown, unruly hair mixed with streaks of gray. Although she met him at a fund raising event years before, she hardly recognized him. Her husband, Don, knew him much better since they played golf together as members of the same country club. Actually, Don recommended him as the guest speaker for Nellie's history class after finding out he was a Vietnam War veteran.

Professor Grainger walked inside. "Mr. Abraham. It's certainly a pleasure meeting you especially after talking a couple of times over the telephone," she said.

"Thank you, Professor; and please call me Kyle. It's nice to meet you, too. I've got to apologize. I wish I didn't have to cancel twice, but my art exhibit in New York kept getting rescheduled. I sincerely apologize."

"Believe me, Kyle, I understand. My husband works for an advertising agency. It seems like he's always on the go. No matter . . . you're here now. I'm so pleased you decided to accept my invitation to speak to my class. They've been studying the Vietnam War for about a week. What say we go up to the lecture hall before the students arrive?"

"Certainly."

"Any questions," Nellie asked, as they walked up the stairs.

"How many students will be in attendance?" Kyle asked.

"About sixty," Nellie said.

"Anything off limits, Professor?"

"Please call me, Nellie; and no, this is a different generation than when you and I were in college. I'm almost ashamed to say, your words may be blasé."

"We'll see," Kyle responded.

Nellie wasn't sure what he meant. She simply brushed it off.

No sooner had they arrived in the lecture hall, the bell rang. Nellie and Kyle made idle conversation as they waited patiently for the next class to arrive. Within minutes every available seat was filled, unusual because several people usually cut class. A guest speaker on a Friday always helped to fill the seats.

After taking attendance, Professor Grainger walked to the side of the class closest the door and said, "Today, it is my pleasure to introduce our guest speaker, Mr. Kyle Abraham." Not remembering Mr. Abraham's wartime credentials, Professor Grainger used an index card as an aid. "In 1969, during the height of the Vietnam War, Mr. Abraham was an infantry soldier stationed with the Fourth Infantry Division in Pleiku. During his tour, he was awarded a Silver Star, a Bronze Star, two Purple Hearts, and numerous other awards and citations." Putting the card down on a student's desk, she addressed the class without using the notes any further. "Mr. Abraham has been a resident of our community for over twenty years, and during that time he has operated his own art gallery and studio; quite a different profession than in his Army days. Mr. Abraham has kindly consented to talk to us today and answer questions about the war. Please afford him your utmost respect and attention." Looking at Kyle, she said, "Mr. Abraham, the floor is yours."

"Thank you, Professor Grainger," Kyle said. "I always enjoy being on campus. It makes me feel young again instead of being . . . years old.

Kyle muffled his voice by briefly covering his mouth to disguise the actual number of years.

Professor Grainger laughed, but many of the students failed to catch his levity.

"Before I start, let me point out some statistics about the war; no, not the war in Iraq, but the one I left behind some thirty-five years ago. Besides the 57,000 plus Americans who were killed in that war — names now inscribed on the Vietnam Memorial in Washington, D.C. — another 303,000 were wounded. Yet, these numbers pale in comparison to the estimated 3,500,000 North and South Vietnamese who were killed or wounded during the ten years of American involvement in that war. That's right: 3,500,000." Kyle paused before continuing. "Think of it in these terms. The entire population of the state of Maryland, man, woman, and child, would be eradicated from the face of the earth. Here's another stat for you to consider: Americans paid (in many cases reluctantly) over $53,000,000,000 to finance the war effort: that's billions, not millions, my friends. Think of all the good that money could have done if spent wisely: on cancer research, world hunger . . . go ahead . . . you name a cause or charity."

A young lady in the front row shed a tear. Kyle didn't expect such a reaction so early in his talk. He considered it a good sign.

"What do you think about those numbers?" Kyle asked. "Come on, what do you honestly think?"

A girl in the third row raised her hand.

"Yes?" Kyle asked.

"It's sad," the girl said. "Your numbers really do put it in perspective, I mean about how terrible the war really was."

"What's your name, Miss?" Kyle asked.

"My name is Nancy . . . Nancy Sawyer."

"Professor Grainger," Kyle said. "Give Nancy Sawyer an 'A'."

Professor Grainger made a gesture as if she was looking for her grade book.

The class laughed. Soon the students settled down, willing to hear more.

Kyle walked from the front of the lecture hall directly up the main aisle before stopping near a young man dressed in a plaid shirt and beige jeans. Looking directly at him, he said, "But there's more to learn you know; much more." Not to embarrass the student further, Kyle scanned the entire class and said, "Folks, this afternoon, I'm not going to talk much about the Vietnam War."

The students and the professor looked puzzled.

"What?" Kyle asked. "Haven't you learned enough about the war from your textbook and all the lectures. I mean, you already know the story, don't you? But being a betting man, I'd wager a ten-spot that none of you know the real outcome: no, not that the war was lost. Heck, everybody knows that. I'm talkin' about what happened to thousands of combat veterans who returned home after the war. Bet you never gave that much thought, now, did you?"

A few students shook their heads. Others stared at Kyle without expression. No one knew what to say, or where he was going with his speech.

"Well, today, ladies and gentlemen, I'm going to write the final chapter right here in front of your very own eyes. With some luck, maybe I'll be able to etch it in your brain. And you know what I'm going to call the final chapter?"

No one responded.

"*Epilogue*. That's what I'm going to call it."

Walking down the ramp to the podium, Kyle pulled out his speech from the inside pocket of his wrinkled blue blazer. The rest of his dress was casual. He wore no tie. His blue jeans were badly faded with an occasional blotch of paint owing to his profession as an artist. His penny loafers, originally black but now gray from not being shined since the day he bought them at a discount department store, were a fair reward for his lack of socks. Giving a final glance at the handwritten speech he labored over for the past several nights, he hoped his talk would be welcome and not far off the mark.

Kyle took a deep breath, sighed, and began his speech. "Those who returned home after living and fighting as caged animals in the enemy infested jungles of Southeast Asia find it difficult, even today, to talk about their wartime exploits. What they witnessed were scenes of unspeakable horror, ghastly images far beyond human comprehension," Kyle said with conviction.

"Please don't take offense to my next statement, okay? I suspect, to you, students of American history, the Vietnam War was just another conflict in a long series of wars. But to combat veterans, it was real, as real as I am standing in front of you today. As for those who served, many are still haunted by gruesome images no less as fresh and painful as if the experience happened yesterday. Far too many are unable to escape the appalling scenes repeatedly played out in their minds, flashbacks that always seem to climax in so much death and destruction. After stepping on a mine or setting off a tripwire, a soldier was blown to smithereens, vaporized in a millisecond. What once was a man was gruesomely transfigured into shredded and smoldering fragments of skin, muscle and bone bearing little resemblance to its previous genetic configuration." Kyle smirked. "Heck, a production line at a midwestern slaughterhouse is far less appalling. At least when cattle are butchered, the procedure is conducted humanely and under rigid sanitary conditions. Until the final dissections, limbs of carcasses are still recognizable as animal appendages."

The lecture hall fell silent.

"Having to view dismemberments and disemboweled entrails was sobering, but it was the expression of the dead that bothered soldiers more, that is, if the face remained intact. The face conveyed a somber message. The stare was expressionless; a lifeless and morbid snapshot of what once was a man. Eyes that remained open were dilated and glazed as if peering into nothingness. Mouths held ajar gave the appearance of a soldier gasping for a final breath. Blood of deep crimson color flowed unchecked from the nose and ears before slowly coagulating as if symbolically conveying a final message: 'I have nothing left to give.

127

Does a similar fate await you?' To combat soldiers, *the look* was terrifying and unforgettable. Let me tell you what I mean, okay?"

No one answered.

"I guess your silence is an indication that I can proceed. Well, let me tell you, those who survived combat thought it blasphemous to look at victims as abstract statistics:

Cpl. Abraham Hellman: gunshot wound to the head; DOA

Sgt. Damian Langley: traumatic amputation of both arms and right leg; loss of blood resulting in death.

Sfc. Benjamin Napier: multiple fragmentation wounds to the upper and lower extremities, death resulting; and

Private Michael Irons: shrapnel through the aorta, death resulting.

To combat soldiers, casualties were more than an alphabetized and categorized list of combat fatalities. Only minutes before, the victims were living . . . breathing . . . swearing . . . smoking . . . bitching . . . loving . . . and . . . laughing, human beings."

Some of the students looked pale. Kyle could sense their discomfort. "I apologize if this is difficult for you, but I feel it has to be said."

Kyle cleared his throat before going on. "That's better," he said. "As early as his first week back in *the World*, that's what we called the States, you know . . . *the World* — as if Vietnam and its inhabitants weren't part of the human race — it was inevitable that someone would ask *the question*, a question just about every combat veteran despised. Perhaps a friend or relative broached the subject. No matter. Whoever asked *the question* was looking for evidence of a soldier's rite of passage, a method of separating the men from the boys, or so they perceived. Those who lived through the wages of war found it difficult to assimilate, much less address," Kyle said.

"By now, you may have already figured out *the question*, the one question you should never ask a combat veteran. What do you think that question is?" Kyle asked the audience.

A young man of about twenty raised his hand.

"Yes," Kyle said.

"What about, 'How does it feel to be so scared?'" he said.

128

"No, that's not the question I was looking for," Kyle said, "but that's a good try, Sir. Who else has a guess?" Kyle asked.

Another gentlemen seating in the back row raised his hand.

"Yes," Kyle said, "but please speak up so we can hear you in the front."

"How about, 'Did you ever kill anyone?'"

"Give that man an 'A,'" Kyle said to no one in particular.

This time there were a few restrained laughs.

Kyle became philosophical. "You know, in my mind, *the question* is thoughtless and disrespectful, probably why veterans shun a direct response. In those rare instances when he does reply, hardly will his answer meet with anyone's satisfaction, either the audience or himself. Here's another way to look at it," Kyle said. "Think of yourself on the receiving end of such a query. Pretend for a moment that you are the main defendant in a court of law. You are being tried for an offense you committed but only carried out in self-defense. The jury is skeptical, and few believe your innocence. The prosecuting attorney has been drilling you unmercifully for an hour, but, whatever the reason, you are not granted the protection of a legal defense team. Psychologically naked and physically isolated during the entire proceeding, you feel defenseless. In your heart you know you are innocent, but no matter what you say continues to be used against you. Facing, what you feel to be, the inevitable; a plea of temporary insanity appears the only recourse. Undoubtedly, those pursuing this line of questioning have already formed an opinion about your guilt or innocence; perhaps worse, they now support an indictment. In their minds, they have already answered the following questions:

I wonder if he enjoyed killing people?
Do you think he's socially maladjusted?
Is he at his breaking point?"

A few students in the audience shook their heads as if to say, *I understand what you're saying.* Kyle was pleased. His message was beginning to be understood.

"Yes! By man's fundamental nature — inquisitive human beings that we are — anything associated with death and the macabre seems to peak our curiosity," he said in a stern voice.

"Strangely — maybe it's not so strange — we find such topics intriguing and worthy of further investigation." He paused to add impact to his next statement. "Regrettably, our society has desensitized itself to the horrors of human suffering." Kyle sighed. "It's a cryin' shame. Don't you agree?"

A few students shook their head in agreement; so did Professor Grainger.

"During combat, a soldier kills to survive, a seemingly enigmatic paradox. Yet, you need not be a combat veteran to understand this contradiction in terms. There is nothing perplexing to comprehend. Fact! An infantryman is trained to kill — killing is a highly practical solution to an unholy profession. Either the soldier kills the enemy or the enemy kills the soldier. There are no gray areas. In combat, killing is an extremely unpleasant but necessary consequence of saving and prolonging one's own human existence. Still . . . taking a life is difficult to rationalize in a civilized society even when that society pleads temporary insanity. Killing, even during combat, seriously erodes nearly everything and anything that a young man has been taught by society about the sanctity of life and what religion has instilled in his soul." Kyle looked at the audience and knew he had them hooked. Looking back down at his speech, he said, "That is why, years later when combat veterans returned home, many questioned their own sanity, morality, and humanity. It's no wonder many chose, and still continue to choose, to remain silent."

A student aggressively waived his hand to ask a question.

Kyle couldn't help but notice. "We have a question," Kyle said.

"Meaning no disrespect, Sir. But did anyone ever ask you that question, and, if so, how did you handle it?" the student said, without making direct eye contact with Kyle.

Kyle thought for a moment considering how best to answer the student. "Well, to be honest," he said, "since my return from Vietnam, I was asked that question a few times over the years. I heard it enough that I became adept at providing a quick answer. Assuming my audience was young or genuinely naïve, like high school students, I usually gave them a stock reply. Although, I may have been brief, evasive and, at times, lied, I tried not to be sarcastic or condescending. These are some of my choice responses:

No, I never shot anyone.

I really don't know. The nights were dark when we made contact. We couldn't see our noses, never mind the enemy.

I prefer not to discuss that aspect of my life. It's just, too, painful.

Can we move on? I'd prefer to talk about healing, not killing."

Kyle brushed his hair back, then provided the student with more information. "I also became well versed at the put-down. I usually reserved these for individuals who honestly deserved what they had coming — stupid question: stupid answer. Consider these:

What kind of a dumb question is that? Next question, please.

You know, I'm glad you asked that question because I actually enjoy reminiscing about such morbid details.

Only God and I need to know the answer to that question. If you're not God, I suggest we move on.

No, I never killed anyone, but I may start now because your question is so incredibly stupid."

Some in the audience giggled. A few held back a laugh.

"And my favorite," Kyle said:

"Be honest! Did your mother ever give birth to a baby that grew up to have even the slightest semblance of intelligence?"

Nearly the entire class burst in laughter.

Kyle had more to say. "Whichever response I chose usually precluded a follow-up question. But you know what?" Kyle said to the student. "Assume for the moment, I gave an honest reply. Doing so could have easily led to the next, yet no less offensive, question. Do you know what that would have been?" he asked.

No one in the class would hazard a guess.

"The next question would have been, *What does it feel like to kill someone?*" Kyle waited to let it sink in. "I suppose the question deserves an answer. Perhaps, by doing so, it will never be asked again, although I doubt it. Here's what I have to say. Many think a soldier experiences a kind of rush when forced to kill. If there is adrenaline, it comes from the inner turmoil and tension of the

131

moment, the fear that you, too, could be killed, not from the taking of another life. Only the well-hardened veteran can put the experience behind him. Some file it away in their unconscious, only to be reminded of the experience years later during flashbacks. Others relive the experience all too often and carry it to their graves."

Kyle looked at his watch and said to the class, "We're running out of time. Let me conclude my talk today by leaving you with a final thought. Military records confirm a well established, but usually unknown fact to the average citizen. Only a small percentage of men sent to Vietnam were infantry soldiers. Even fewer actually recorded a kill. The majority were support troops who served in the rear. The only thing they killed were a few cases of beer and countless mosquitoes."

The audience laughed.

"Bona fide infantrymen — *grunts* — are in the minority. If you do meet one someday, let me say emphatically: 'Let them be!' Should they want to discuss their combat exploits, they will breach the topic. And if and when you feel the urge to ask *the question*, I strongly recommend you resist the temptation. Instead, I offer you a more pertinent question, one with only positive connotations that will, most likely, win you a friend. That is: "Did anyone ever say to you, 'Thank you for serving your country?'""

"Thanks for having me, and I hope my little speech today wasn't that disappointing."

Professor Grainger stood and clapped. It wasn't long before the entire class was standing and joined in the applause.

An Artist's Hands; A Combat Veteran's Soul

THE CROWNING GLORY

It is a far, far better thing that I do, than I have ever done;
it is a far, far better rest I go to, than I have ever known.
-Charles Dickens, *A Tale of Two Cities* (1859)

F ire Support Base Alfa (a Marine outpost 27 miles
northwest of Da Nang)
July 16, 1967
0105 hours
The Attack

The portable radio remained on long after the station's sign-off. Only intermittent static and the serenade of chirping insects buffeted the tomblike silence of the night.

Sergeant James McElroy, a draftee from the Piedmont area of North Carolina, had been groovin' to the faded radio signal of a Beatles recording, "If I Needed Someone," spun by a rear-echeloned disk jockey assigned to the safe confines of an air-conditioned studio. Accompanying the tune, McElroy's rendition nearly drowned out the Fab Four. But to him, it really didn't matter. Anything he could do to take his mind off the nightmare he faced each day was fine by him. Da Nang was distant, but the World, as he remembered it, seemed light-years away.

While in base camp, McElroy followed the same late-evening ritual — he'd listen to a little rock 'n' roll, smoke a joint, fantasize about the girls back home, perhaps write a letter or two, then doze off until early morning only to be awakened by an eardrum-piercing scream, a loud and monstrous howl that became all too familiar: "Rise and shine all you lucky people. It's gonna be another beautiful day in exotic South Vietnam!"

McElroy's tent-mates were manning perimeter bunkers for the night and, to him, the implication was self-evident: the entire four-man shelter was his exclusive domain, that is, at least until morning. Sprawling on his cot, he remained motionless. This is the life, man! Tonight they'll be no snoring or bitching to contend with.

134

Lackadaisically, he placed his hands behind his head and stared at the emptiness of the water-stained ceiling as he let out a muffled groan of contentment. It wasn't long before he lapsed into an intoxicating sleep.

Less than an hour passed before McElroy was unceremoniously jolted awake by a deafening explosion . . . wham . . . followed a millisecond later by a brilliant flash of light. The intensity and close proximity of the blast diffused the light so the canvas tent projected an x-ray image of a mountain range more than half a mile away

Explosions continued to reverberate, rocking the ground like a California tremor. "Holy shit!" he shouted even though nobody could hear him. The enemy left little doubt about their intention: by destroying the main gate with mortars and disabling the main defensive bunkers, a wave of advancing enemy could waltz unscathed through the compound inflicting unspeakable havoc upon the small contingent of Marines guarding the outpost.

Minute to medium-size fragments of shrapnel and coarse gravel jettisoned into the sky only moments before began to rain down from the heavens. Debris fell everywhere including on McElroy's humble abode. He couldn't help but wonder that it sounded just like rain. Though groggy from the abrupt wake-up, he knew better — the monsoons weren't scheduled to arrive for several months.

He had few options. Instinctively, he rolled from his cot onto the damp ground. Trying to slither under it, he struck his forehead on the side of one of four concrete blocks placed there as additional elevation to protect against poisonous snakes and plague-carrying rodents. "Damn!" he muttered under his breath as he rubbed his head. Dazed but a moment, he regained his composure. Lying face down, he stretched out his left arm and pulled the thin, discolored mattress off the cot and over his body. Whether it offered any protection was debatable. During Infantry Training Reserve, he was instructed to follow this simple procedure. Under the present circumstances, he wasn't about to question its merit. When another round hit precariously close to his shelter, he let out a bloodcurdling scream: "Incoming!" The warning fell on deaf ears. By now, everyone was wide-awake and well aware of the threatening situation about to unfold.

No sooner did the word depart his lips then guys began scrambling from their tents, searching for the protection of the closest bunker. McElroy's mind was processing data at warp speed. Half-crazed, he thought, *I better make a break for it before it's too late.* Without hesitation, he leaped to his feet, picked up his flak jacket and helmet and threw them on. Grabbing two bandoleers of magazines filled with M-16 rounds, he slung them over his head and underneath each arm. After securing his rifle, he unlaced the opening of the tent. Dashing out, he headed toward the closest bunker less than 30 yards away. Within several feet of the opening, he leaped forward and slid headfirst. After pushing himself up to his hands and knees, he crawled the remaining distance into the bunker.

Suddenly another round hit . . . wham. The concussion of the blast slammed him to the ground.

Crack. Crack.

The distinct sound of enemy small arms fire from AK-47 rifles continued to intensify. McElroy thought, *Damn it! We're dead meat!* Pulling himself up, he looked out through a makeshift opening in the wall. The sky was ablaze in colors — greens, reds and yellows. Guards manning the eight perimeter bunkers surrounding the compound were firing hand-held flares. McElroy could hear the sounds clearly. Whoosh . . . whoosh as the illuminating devices rocketed toward the heavens. Seconds later he heard noises: pop . . . pop as the silk parachutes opened to reveal the pyrotechnic display. After gliding in an easterly direction for approximately 200 yards while gradually descending toward earth, the flares extinguished themselves but only after sputtering like a child's sparkler on the Fourth of July. The guards had detected movement in the free-fire zone outside the perimeter wire and needed the light to detect the enemy. As usual, it was only wishful thinking. Knowing the enemy was in close proximity was one thing, but seeing him was another — about as difficult as winning the Irish Sweepstakes on a pound wager.

Besides McElroy, five others made it to the bunker — Sergeant John 'Slick' Vendetti, Lance Corporals Michael 'Jiggs' Sinclair, John 'Dale' Ives, Leonard 'Frenchie' LeBeau, and Private First

Class Ralph 'Ralphie' Nugent. All were seasoned combat veterans each with over six months in country.

Seconds passed before Lieutenant Shawn Kendall came running in. Catching his breath, he asked, "Is everyone okay?"

Vendetti answered for all. "We're all right, Lieutenant."

"Good!" said the Lieutenant. "Now listen up! I need all of you as reinforcements at the eastern perimeter. That end's taking a hell of a pounding. Any questions? . . . No? All right then, get yourself into high gear and make a run for it."

Nobody asked why. There wasn't a need. Lieutenant Kendall led the way, followed close behind by McElroy, Vendetti, and the others. Mortars continued to explode at the east end of the compound. All seven Marines were running directly toward a hellish barrage.

After arriving safely, each man realized he would be afforded only the bare necessities. Crudely constructed, the bunker was nothing more than a double-stacked row of sandbags, or what was left of them. Over time, the green nylon sacks had split and oozed their precious contents onto the barren ground. An occasional breeze finished the job, spreading the loose granules over a wide area. The breastwork was only four feet high and eight feet wide while the sidewalls tapered down from four feet in the front to less than two in the rear. The fortification faced toward the east. Unlike the perimeter bunker, this complex was air-conditioned — there was no roof. Designed as a transitory shelter for defensive maneuvering, it was situated only yards behind a more ruggedly constructed wood and sandbag fortification near the main perimeter gate.

Fifty yards in front was a row of razor-sharp concertina wire with an ingeniously designed, yet inexpensive early-warning system — empty aluminum Budweiser and Coca-Cola cans tied to the wire. The working theory was elementary. Should the enemy attempt to cut through the wire during darkness, the clanking noise caused by the cans banging together would alert the guards. In principle, the hypothesis appeared sound. In practice, the primitive configuration of wire and cans would only succeed if there were no other distractions. But there were distractions. The simplistic alarm system was no match for the deafening noise of mortar and rocket explosions and small arms fire; that which preceded a full-scale ground attack. Intrinsically flawed from the start, 'Nam was full of such placebos; regrettably, it usually resulted in untimely deaths.

By now the Marines were painfully aware of their predicament. There was little, if anything, they could do.

"Where the hell is Clarence?" yelled Vendetti. Clarence was the anointed nickname of a 23-pound, M-60 machine gun that was normally mounted inside the bunker.

"Yesterday, the Captain ordered me to move it to the other side of the compound," McElroy replied.

"Why would he tell you that?"

"The machine gun in the west bunker kept jammin' and it needed maintenance. I guess he figured, if we got attacked, it'd be there."

"Well . . . he fuckin' figured wrong. Now what the hell are we suppose to do?" Vendetti bellowed.

McElroy remained expressionless. What could he say? It wasn't his fault. After all, he was only following orders.

Meanwhile, Lieutenant Kendall glanced over the bunker. "Damn!" he exclaimed, not realizing his men could hear him. After evaluating the situation, he slid back down. Looking at the small group he said, "The main perimeter's been breached. E-2's taken a direct hit."

"What'll we do?" yelled Vendetti.

"We can't let a damn soul come through the wire! You hear me? Not a damn soul!"

It didn't take long before Vendetti became inquisitive as he guardedly peered over the sandbags. Shocked, he couldn't believe his eyes. Despite the relative darkness, he could see figures crawling through a four-foot-wide breach in the concertina wire. The spiral obstruction now resembled a porous sponge. Goose bumps instantaneously appeared on his arms.

"Lieutenant! Lieutenant!" he screamed. "There's gooks crawling through the wire!"

"You sure?" Kendall yelled back.

"Sure as hell, Lieutenant!" Vendetti said, his eyes nearly bulging from their sockets.

"Set your weapons on full automatic," Kendall ordered, "and whatever you do, keep your aim low and away from E-2. The last thing we want is to shoot one of our own. When I tell you to let him have it, empty your magazines." Seconds later he commanded: "Fire!"

Perched with heads and rifles barely visible above the sandbags, the men fired their weapons toward the darkness ahead. One hundred and twenty rounds of ammunition were expended in less than three seconds. The trajectory of the bullets covered nearly every conceivable angle where the perimeter had been breached. Still, Lieutenant Kendall was skeptical. "Lock and load!" he ordered a second time. Nobody needed encouragement. Using the palm of his hand, each man slammed another magazine into his rifle while pulling back on the slide bolt with his thumb and forefinger to chamber a round.

"Get ready," yelled the Lieutenant.

"Fire!"

Rat-tat-tat. Rat-tat-tat.

The crescendo of rifle-fire quickly subsided. Each man had emptied a second magazine of 5.56-millimeter rounds. A sane individual would argue it impossible for any fallible being to survive such a hellish barrage; yet, someone had. Small, but deadly, projectiles continued to be fired from outside the perimeter.

Whap . . . whap.

Stray bullets drilled into the sandbags quickly lost velocity before coming to an abrupt halt. The compactness of the sand served its intended purpose but not before the rounds gave each man a bone chilling fright.

After firing two consecutive volleys on full automatic, each man's flash suppresser at the end of the rifle barrel briefly turned yellowish-orange. Lieutenant Kendall was aware that another such ploy could cause the barrels to overheat and distort, making them useless.

Someone had to look up again, but all feared the unthinkable. Despite the darkness — there was moonlight — each knew he could become a target or, even worse, a candidate for the morgue. Sharpshooters were not the main concern. The thought of being hit by stray bullets bothered them more. During a typical skirmish, misguided rounds could take as many lives as accurate and concentrated gunfire. The anxiety of being killed this way was a fear men on both sides of the line could not forget. It was about as unceremonious and inglorious a way for any soldier to depart this world. No warrior, friend or foe, deserved it.

During a brief lull, Vendetti and McElroy worked up enough courage to peer over the sandbags. They saw movement, but only McElroy heard what he believed to be faint voices emanating from the distance. Quickly they slid down the sandbagged wall, welcoming the protection and intimacy of their bunker.

"Lieutenant!" shouted McElroy. "I hear voices."

"Are you sure?" asked Kendall.

"I think so," said McElroy, but he sounded a little less certain than seconds before. "Let me check again, Lieutenant!"

"Go ahead," said the lieutenant, "but make it quick."

"What, Lieutenant?" McElroy asked.

"I said, "Do it fast, and don't let yourself become a target!""

McElroy raised his left hand in acknowledgement. Slowly he lifted his head over the wall. At first, all was quiet. Listening intently, he heard the same faint voice or voices he thought he heard earlier. He was unable to make out any of them.

Mortars continued to slam into the compound. When McElroy heard the explosions, he jerked his head down. Seconds later, he was back peering over the sandbags.

"Help me . . . please help me!" came a feeble cry out of the darkness.

McElroy heard the distress call. Looking out, he tried to localize the sound.

"God, please help me!" came a louder plea.

This time, McElroy heard it clearly. He was sure about that but less certain of what he thought he saw lying on the ground. The night sky did not help. Suddenly, an aerial flair drifted by and illuminated the area. McElroy saw a shadowy figure rolling back and forth near the bunker. Others lay motionless nearby.

Lieutenant Kendall became impatient and, in one single yank, grabbed McElroy by the fatigue jacket and pulled him down. "Did you hear anything?" he asked.

"Yeah! One of our guys is still alive, maybe more."

"Where?"

"Someone's on the ground a few feet from the bunker."

"Can we get to him?" the lieutenant asked.

McElroy shook his head. "No way."

"What?" said the lieutenant. "Damn it, speak louder! I can't hear you."

McElroy yelled over the ground fire, "No way, Lieutenant! It'd be damn near suicide!"

Lance Cpl. John 'Dale' Ives, nervously chewing a stick of Juicy Fruit gum, asked the lieutenant, "Isn't anyone going to help 'em?"

"We've got to wait for reinforcements," said the lieutenant.

"But, Lieutenant," cried Dale, "they'll never last out there."

"We've got no choice," said the lieutenant.

Dale lifted himself up off the ground and peered over the sandbags. After surveying the situation he fell to his knees. "Lieutenant," he said. "Let me go out there and get 'em."

Lieutenant Kendall was quick to respond. "No way! I can't afford to lose any of you."

"But Lieutenant!"

"No! And that's an order."

When it came to Dale, what you saw was what you got. His amiable qualities were deeply ingrained in his personality. Whenever the chaplain said Mass, Dale served as an altar boy. When someone was melancholy, Dale was there to lend support. It was evident; he would give the shirt off his back to help his fellow man. Everyone loved him.

Dale was facing a mind-boggling dilemma; torn between following the order of a superior officer or doing what he thought was morally right. Unarmed, and without further thought, he rolled over the right side of the bunker, picked himself up, and ran in the direction of the fallen soldier. The flash of distant mortar explosions temporarily blinded him. Bullets sailed through the air like whistling wind, invisible but deadly if they hit their mark.

141

Undaunted, Dale darted toward the now visible figure, zigzagging until a much closer mortar blast knocked him to the ground. Uninjured except for an incredible ringing in his ears, he picked himself up and continued his mission. Within five yards of the wounded Marine, he jumped feet first and slid beside the stricken Marine.

"Can ya get up? If you can, I'll carry ya back," Dale said to the Marine.

"I'll try," came the feeble response.

Lifting the unidentified Marine, Dale took the brunt of his weight upon his shoulders. Quickly, he trotted toward the bunker directly ahead of him. Dale could hear the whizzing bullets. Luckily, they missed. Only yards from the bunker, Dale and the wounded Marine stumbled and fell. Seeing what was happening, Vendetti and Nugent ran out to assist. Within seconds, the Marine had been carried to relative safety.

Before another word was spoken, Dale bolted into the darkness for a second time. His destination was a downed Marine less than 35 yards to the northeast. This time bullets did not impede his progress. After diving to the ground, Dale crawled a short distance to the stricken Marine.

"Can ya stand?" he asked. There was no response. Checking the Marine's vital signs, Dale figured he was still alive, although barely. There was no alternative. Dale would have to carry the soldier back to safety. Slinging him over his right shoulder, he sluggishly carried the dead weight toward the bunker. Before making any headway, a round careened off his left forearm. Though the wound left only a small gash, the impact was enough to spin Dale completely around, forcing him to lose his balance. Remarkably, he held his footing. Scrambling the final yards to safety, he rolled the wounded Marine off his shoulder. Lieutenant Kendall and Vendetti each helped to pull the limp body into the bunker.

Injured and with his energy nearly spent, Dale lay motionless on his stomach just outside the bunker.

"Grab my hand," Jiggs yelled.

Dale stuck out his arm as Jiggs pulled him over the side.

"You crazy fool!" yelled the lieutenant. "You could have been killed."

After catching his breath, Dale responded, "I know, Lieutenant . . . I know."

Nugent wrapped Dale's foreman with a large bandage taken from Dale's own web belt. The wound was superficial, yet still painful.

During a lull in the fighting, Frenchie thought he heard someone. The sound was emanating from an area several yards away near the breached perimeter wire. Frenchie again listened intently. Within seconds he recognized the inflection of the voice. "Lieutenant!" he yelled. "There's someone else alive out there, and I don't think it's one of ours."

"What the hell are you saying?" asked the lieutenant.

"Lieutenant . . . I think it's a gook."

"Are you sure?"

"I don't know, it's hard to . . ."

Jiggs interrupted. "Lieutenant, should we waste 'em?"

"Not so fast," said the lieutenant. "We're not certain who it is. What if, just what if he's one of ours?"

Dale overheard the conversation while trying to regain what little remained of his strength.

Dale respected life to the fullest. The love he nurtured and showered upon his fellow man transcended all social, cultural, economic, and racial boundaries. It was his upbringing that prepared him well — Dale's father was a Lutheran minister; and though he had no wish to follow in his father's footsteps, he practiced his religion faithfully. At base camp, it was not uncommon to see Dale reading the Bible after evening chow. Dale's only vice, if you could call it such, was an affinity for chewing gum. It was a compulsion, not much different from those who smoke cigarettes, but his habit was healthier.

"What should we do, Lieutenant?" Frenchie asked.

"Let me think a second," he responded.

Before the lieutenant could decide, Dale's mind was already made up: It's a human being out there, maybe an American. I've got to do somethin'. If I don't, I'll never be able to live with myself. Pulling himself to his knees, he looked out over the bunker. He saw what Frenchie had seen, a shadow of a man on the ground west of the breached perimeter. But the voice was silent. Dale sensed it would take a Herculean effort to accomplish the rescue. Bloodied but unbowed, he used the sandbags to guide himself to his feet. Rolling over the bunker, he pushed himself up and dashed straight ahead looking more like a drunken sailor than a well-conditioned Marine.

"Corporal!" the lieutenant yelled at the top of his lungs. "Get back here, you crazy son-of-a-bitch!"

Dale heard the lieutenant but disregarded the order. *It's too late to turn back*, he thought. The commitment had been made.

As Dale continued his stumbling run, he said a short prayer: Lord, help me! Please give me the strength to finish the job.

As the prayer left his lips, a mortar exploded less than 40 yards to his left. A few small pieces of shrapnel tore into his left shoulder. Another piece ripped into his cheek splitting the top of two teeth before lodging in the roof of his mouth. The concussion of the blast knocked him off his feet and onto his right side.

"Damn it!" Dale exclaimed, as he lay dazed on the ground. While spitting up blood, his ears began to ring.

Lieutenant Kendall witnessed the gruesome scene unfold as the moonlit sky aided his vision.

"What's wrong, Lieutenant?" asked Vendetti.

"The corporal's down. That last shell got him. Wait . . . wait a minute. I think he's trying to get up. He is, God damn it! Nugent! McElroy! Give him some cover."

Crack. Crack. . . . crack. The sound of rifle fire echoed throughout the perimeter.

By now, Dale had managed to regain his senses. With all his resolve, he rolled onto his knees, and then fumbled back to his feet. Somehow he managed to sprint the final distance without further injury, although occasional rounds passed precariously close to his body.

Using his good arm, he pulled the injured man onto his side. Frenchie was right, he speculated. He's Vietnamese. Dale was staring directly into the face of a Viet Cong sapper. Except for a

144

loincloth, the man was naked. Putting his ear to the enemy's lips, he detected a moaning sound accompanied by what seemed like Vietnamese gibberish.

All the while, the soldier's eyes remained open but appeared incredibly distant. "*Me . . . Me!*" the soldier cried. He was calling for his mother, Dale believed.

"Thank God! You're alive," Dale said out loud.

Pulling his hand back from the soldier's body, Dale felt slime. Instinctively, he wiped the substance onto his fatigues. Dale was oblivious at the time, but his hand had come in contact with free-flowing blood. The sapper was shot in the hip. The high caliber round exited through the man's thigh, leaving a large gaping wound.

The VC was falling in and out of consciousness. Dale pried his bad arm under the soldier's neck and lifted it slightly. Pulling his canteen off his web belt, he offered the soldier a drink of water, using words from his meager Vietnamese vocabulary: "*Do uong. Do uong!*" The soldier took a small swig but gagged and vomited. Dale decided to pour water into his right hand and allow the VC to drink from it. Placing it near the enemy's mouth, he said again "*Do uong. Do uong!*"

The VC took a sip, coughed once but managed to retain the precious liquid.

"*Chung ta hay!*" Dale told the soldier. Lacking skills of a Vietnamese linguist, he gave the language his best shot. In English, what Dale tried to say in Vietnamese was, "Let's get out of here."

Ignoring his own wounds, Dale pulled the soldier into a sitting position then lifted him the best he could. The VC moaned in agony. Without thinking, he slung him over his right shoulder. Dale struggled to carry him approximately fifteen yards before losing what little strength he possessed before tumbling face first to the ground. He landed with the dead weight of the VC falling directly upon him. Lucky for Dale, the ground was soft sand.

Periodically poking their heads above the bunker, all five men witnessed the unfolding event. Although incoming mortar rounds had stopped, nobody dared leave the sanctuary of their bunker as occasional enemy sniper rounds still penetrated the air.

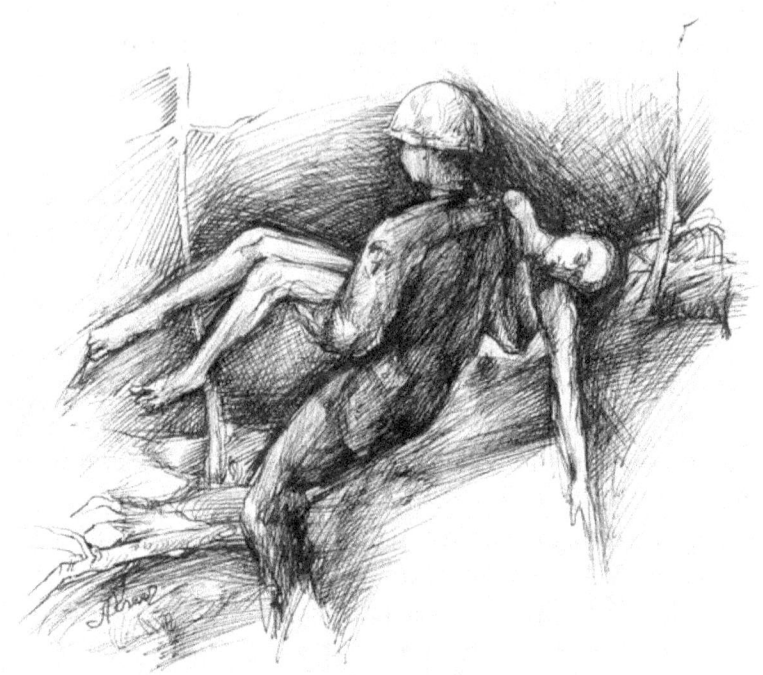

Dale Rescues an Enemy Soldier

No words were spoken. They watched as an agonizing and astonishing scene unfolded before them.

Lying on top of the VC to protect him from further harm, Dale spit blood and sand from his mouth. Desperately, he tried to get up. He couldn't. All his strength was drained. Positioning himself onto his side so he could roll the soldier on top of his own stomach, he grabbed the VC under the armpits and pulled him over. Slowly he began the long and laborious crawl toward the defensive bunker. Using his legs, he pushed as best he could against the sand. The pain in his arm and shoulder intensified. The trek was excruciating and slow.

Vendetti couldn't take it any longer. He turned toward Nugent and said, "We've got to help him."

"I know," Nugent replied.

"Lieutenant, what da ya think?" Vendetti asked. "Dale's in trouble. He needs our help."

Almost without thinking, the lieutenant responded. "Listen up! You three," the lieutenant pointed directly at Vendetti, Nugent, and LeBeau, "and I will go after them. Sergeant! You and I will take the corporal. LeBeau! You and the private handle the other guy. Corporal! You stay here and give us cover. Any questions?"

Silence prevailed.

"All right. Is everyone ready?"

Each nodded.

"All right . . . Let's go, let's go, let's go!" he yelled as they jumped over the sides of the bunker.

Immediately, concentrated enemy sniper fire came from the jungle. The source was difficult to localize. A few rounds hit the ground to LeBeau's right, kicking up small clouds of dust, but not one hit its intended target.

The run was brief, only 20 to 25 yards.

Seconds later, the rescue team was kneeling over the fallen men. Picking them up and slinging their arms over their shoulders, they shuffled back to the bunker. No more than
five to six strides away from relative safety, an enemy round struck LeBeau in the right calf. He buckled over as if hit by a baseball bat, taking down Nugent and the VC soldier.

"Shit, man, I'm hit!" LeBeau cried out in excruciating pain.

"Can ya get up?" Nugent asked.

"I don't know, damn it. I think my leg is pretty screwed up." Clinching his teeth in agony, he said, "Gimme a second and I'll try."

Nugent took the response as a positive sign. *We've got to get under cover before our asses get blown away*, Nugent surmised. Regaining his footing, he looked at LeBeau and said, "It's now or never, man."

"Okay," LeBeau responded. "Help me up."

Nugent grabbed LeBeau under each shoulder blade and pulled him to his feet. After steadying him, Nugent picked up the VC and swung him toward LeBeau. No words were spoken. Though severely wounded, LeBeau made every effort to carry his fair share of the weight. Laboriously, both men dragged the enemy soldier between them, LeBeau limping and swaying with every step. After reaching the bunker, and without warning, LeBeau collapsed. Nugent was left standing with the full weight of the VC resting upon his shoulder. Leaning to his side, he rolled the prisoner in an upright position against the bunker. Vendetti, who had just arrived moments before with Dale and the lieutenant, pulled the prisoner over the sandbags. Lieutenant Kendall, seeing what was happening, and realizing nobody was helping LeBeau, grabbed him by the collar of his bulletproof vest and yanked him over the wall.

Within five minutes, the attack ended. The events were markedly similar to how it all began forty minutes earlier. At first, everything was silent. Suddenly, Marines scurried around the compound. Finally, officers barked commands.

USS Sanctuary (anchored off the coast of Da Nang in the
  South China Sea)
July 17, 1967
1400 Hours
The Aftermath

All the wounded, including the sapper, were medevac'd to a hospital ship. In spite of all that Dale experienced, he suffered few

148

ill effects. His forearm was cleaned, stitched, and dressed by a physician. The flesh wound needed eight stitches to close. Small pieces of shrapnel that had lodged in his shoulder were removed during a routine surgical procedure. The shrapnel that pierced his cheek and mouth were extracted during the same operation. Only a few stitches were required to mend each wound. As for his cracked teeth, Dale would need the services of a dentist to have them capped, though there was no urgency to schedule a visit. As for Dale's ears, a preliminary examination revealed a slight hearing loss. The medical prognosis was highly favorable: Rest for three weeks, then return to duty.

Leonard 'Frenchie' LeBeau was not as fortunate. The wound in his calf was examined by several physicians and diagnosed as serious. Because of the large loss of muscle tissue, the prognosis was poor. Doctors felt he would eventually be able to walk again but not without a noticeable limp. For stability, Frenchie was told he'd have to use a cane for the rest of his life. The first operation was performed that morning. After the surgery the doctors advised Frenchie that he'd require three to four more skin grafts back in the States. His days in combat were numbered. Frenchie was ecstatic.

The first Marine Dale carried to safety suffered multiple fragmentation wounds to the face, chest, and forearms. Shrapnel seriously damaged the Marine's right eye and the probability that sight would return was unlikely. Amazingly, no single wound was considered life threatening. The patient was given sufficient medication to lessen his immediate discomfort. The medical prognosis: Because of the seriousness of the eye injury and other wounds requiring skin grafts, the patient is to be shipped to Japan within the next forty-eight hours.

The second Marine Dale rescued was connected to a life-support system. The soldier was in grave condition. Shrapnel had torn clear through his groin and intestines. The next forty-eight hours would be a better indicator of his chances for survival.

The enemy soldier was immediately placed in intensive care. Less than an hour later, lying between other seriously wounded Marines, he succumbed. There was little the doctors could do in spite of working frantically to maintain his vital signs. The severe loss of blood proved fatal.

Battalion Headquarters, Da Nang
Office of Colonel Edward P. Mallinson
September 2, 1967
0900 Hours

"Colonel. Lance Corporal Ives reporting as ordered, Sir!" said Dale, snapping to attention as he saluted.

Colonel Mallinson returned the salute. "At ease, Corporal." Slowly lifting himself up from the chair, he walked around the olive-green, steel desk and stood but a few feet from Dale. Looking him squarely in the eyes, he said, "I've ordered you here today to discuss a few important issues. You understand what I'm saying, Corporal?"

"Yes, Sir!" Dale said in typical Marine Corps fashion. Truthfully, Dale hadn't the foggiest clue why he had been summoned.

Colonel Mallinson was odd, perhaps demented. His build was that of a Sherman tank — short, rugged, and ready for a fight, on or off the battlefield. As for the rest of his appearance, he looked every bit a consummate Marine. But posing as a pillar of strength was more a façade than an established fact. In many ways, he resembled a glass door: you could see right through him, but if you inadvertently ran into him, you were likely to become seriously injured. As a leader, he lacked the entire repertoire of qualifying attributes: empathy, compassion, and the ability to gain and retain the respect of his men. Indicative of a failed genetic experiment, his personality was a cross between an obsessed dreamer, a caged animal, and a registered lunatic. During his tour, he was nothing more than an obscure bit player in the unfolding drama, driven incessantly by his own feelings of self-importance. Many, from peers to higher-ranking officers, thought him to be a quintessential moron with a reptilian brain. Ironically, his superiors possessed short memories, as he always seemed to be in the right place at the right time when promotions were given. For him, the war was a blessing in disguise as it prolonged his less than illustrious career.

"I've just completed reading the after-battle report along with other corroborating statements about the engagement last month at the fire base," said the colonel, pausing for a moment. "Corporal, because of you, I've lost some damn important Marine Corps property. Corporal LeBeau is out of commission. He's been medevac'd back to the States. You understand what I'm saying, Corporal?"

"Sir?"

With a priggish expression that appeared permanently laminated to his face, Colonel Mallinson continued to rip into the corporal. "Corporal Ives. Because of you, I'm short a man at a time when I can't afford to lose any more of *my* Marines. And that's not the half of it," he said, raising his voice while seething. "You disobeyed a direct order from a superior officer. Lieutenant Kendall ordered you to remain in the bunker, yet you disobeyed his command. Is that right, Corporal?"

"Yes, Sir, I did."

"Dare I ask, Why?" Colonel Mallinson inquired with a touch of sarcasm.

"I didn't think it was right to abandon a wounded man on the field, Sir."

"Corporal. You're not supposed to think. That's why the Corps has officers. Listen to me, Corporal. If that's not bad enough, I lost a valuable Marine so you could save a God damned gook." Suddenly, the colonel's face reddened and the veins in his forehead bulged. "You're a Marine, God damn it. You've been trained to kill the enemy, not save 'em!"

"I know, Sir, but . . ."

"No buts, Corporal. You screwed up royally. You understand what I'm saying?"

"Yes, Sir. I screwed up."

After a moment, Colonel Mallinson looked directly into Dale's eyes and said, "Lieutenant Kendall recommended you for an important decoration. Did you know that corporal?"

"No, Sir, I didn't."

"Corporal. You're lucky I don't bust your sorry ass, never mind endorsing you for a God-damned decoration. Corporal Ives? You've dishonored the Corps! You know that, don't you?" Not waiting for an answer, he continued his tirade. "You see this recommendation?" as he waved then dangled it inches from Dale's face.

"Yes, Sir, I do."

"Well, now you don't!" he said ripping it into small pieces and tossing it like confetti into the wastebasket adjacent his desk.

"I've got some advice for you, Corporal. Straighten out your act, and be a Marine! This time, I'm letting you off easy. I could have busted you down to private. Now, get out of my face!"

"Yes, Sir," Dale said, his head hanging low because of the colonel's unexpected tongue-lashing.

"What's that, Corporal?"

"Yes, Sir!" Dale said again, this time with superfluous emotion. He followed it up with a snappy salute.

"That's better," said the colonel, as he returned the salute. "Now get out of my office, go back to your unit, and think about our little conversation!"

Winston-Salem, North Carolina
32 Years Later
7:10 p.m. (EST)

"Honey! The phone's ringing. Could you pick it up? I'm in the bathroom."

"No problem, Abby, I'll get it," responded James as he walked into the kitchen and toward the wall phone. He picked up the receiver after the fourth ring, just quick enough to avoid the answering machine from recording the call. "Hello!" he said.

Dead silence prevailed. James felt ill at ease, like someone was listening but wouldn't respond. "Hello!" he said again. After a few more seconds, he heard a soft-spoken voice barely audible on the other end of the line.

"Is this James?"

"Yes, this is James."

"James McElroy?"

"Yes, this is James . . . James McElroy." Figuring it was another telemarketer, he prepared to hang up, but before he did, his curiosity got the best of him.

"Are you the same James McElroy that was stationed with the Third Marines at Fire Support Base Alpha late in 1967; a guy nicknamed 'Red'?"

"Who is this?" James inquired.

"I'm sorry. I should have introduced myself sooner. Does the name Ralph Nugent ring a bell?"

"My God! Ralphie! Certainly I remember you. How the hell are you?"

"I'm all right. How are you?"

"I'm doing fine. How'd you find me? I never figured I'd be hearing from any of you guys again in a million years. Gees! After all, it's been over 30 somethin' years."

"You know, Red, the Web's a wonderful thing. I just looked up your name on-line using the White Pages and through a process of elimination . . . well, to make a long story short, here I am. You don't mind if I still call you Red, do you?"

"Hell no! But what possessed you to call after so many years? Don't get me wrong. I'm thrilled to hear your voice. But I'm curious."

"Remember Dale . . . Dale Ives?"

"You mean the 'Juicy Fruit Kid'? How could I forget him?"

"We both came from the same state. Did you know that?" asked Ralph.

"No, I didn't," said James.

"Yeah. He was from South Hadley, Massachusetts. I came from Hyannis, the opposite end of the state. When we got out of the service, we kept in touch. After 'Nam, I visited him on several occasions, all for good reason. I became close to his family, so close, that I married his sister." Ralph chuckled as he said, "Dale's my brother-in-law."

"No kidding!" said James. "That's great!"

"Thanks. Yup! He's been my brother-in-law for over 25 years. When Diane and I were having marital difficulties, Dale and his wife, Sandy, helped us work things out. I'll never forget them for that."

"That's great, but I've got to admit, I'm not surprised. He's one of those rare individuals who looked out for the other guy before taking care of himself."

"That's for sure, Red, and that's why we need to talk."

"What's up?"

"A few months ago, Dale and Sandy came over to visit my wife and me. It wasn't the kind of visit we expected. They brought disturbing news. As Sandy tells it, for weeks Dale was experiencing a recurring fever and night sweats. In less than a month, he had lost nearly 25 pounds. One morning while shaving, he noticed his lymph nodes had swollen. Later that morning, with Sandy's persistence, Dale was coaxed into consulting a doctor at UMass Memorial Health Care Center in Worcester. You see, Dale is an associate professor in the history department at UMASS Amherst. Two days later, he went through a battery of tests. The results were staggering, and the prognosis bleak."

"What was it?"

"Dale was diagnosed with cancer — non-Hodgkin's lymphoma. The doctor suspected it may have been caused by exposure to Agent Orange in 'Nam. Who knows? But when you think about it, Red, we were all exposed to that damn chemical. In the end, it'll probably kill more of us than did the enemy."

"What can I do?" asked James. "Does he need money for an operation? How much does he need? Tell me. What can I..."

Ralph interrupted. "Red! It's not a question of money, and an operation won't help. His illness is terminal. But there is somethin' we can do before all of his tomorrows are past."

"And what's that?" James asked.

"To right a terrible wrong."

"What terrible wrong?"

Remember the night Dale saved those guys?"

"Ralphie, how can I ever forget that night and what he did?"

"Neither can I. Do you know what he got for his bravery?"

"As far as I was concerned, he deserved the Medal of Honor."

"Same here, Red. But you know what he ended up with?

"No . . . what?"

"The shaft! He got nothin' — no awards, no congratulations, not a friggin' thing. Wait a minute. I take that back. He did get a Purple Heart. After that all he got was a shit load of grief."

"You're kidding? I figured at the very least he'd get a Silver Star. Ralphie, I don't know if you remember, but my tour ended less than a month after that attack. Tell me what happened?"

Ralph continued to tell James the entire, despicable story.

"After recovering from his wounds, Dale was called into Colonel Mallinson's office only to be reprimanded and then belittled. Dale never got over the humiliation from the colonel's dress-down. That pompous ass forever tainted his tour of duty and his bravery. Adding insult to injury, it came from a service Dale, and the rest of us held in such high esteem, one for which Dale was willing to die."

"I had no idea. Never in a million years would I have imagined such a thing."

"Red, I've let this go unresolved far too long. I should have done somethin' sooner. Because of Dale's present medical condition, I'm committed to taking care of this matter once and for all. We've got to act, and act now before it's too late. We've got to get Dale the recognition he so justly deserves."

"I agree," said James. "But what can we do? I mean, it happened so many years ago."

"I've already done the homework. I've contacted my senator and talked for hours with members of his staff. Their advice has been invaluable. They told me to get certified affidavits from at least two veterans who witnessed Dale's heroics, preferably more. If you're willing, you'll be one of them. I'll be another."

"Of course I will! How about the other guys? Have you located anyone else?"

"Red, believe it or not, I've located nearly every guy that was there that night. Unfortunately, Jiggs died several years ago. Last week, over the telephone, I talked to his sister for a long while. The way she tells it, Vietnam ate him up inside. He just couldn't let it go. He died of liver failure. Ya know, I honestly loved that guy."

"That's too bad. So did I. He was an absolute peach. Jiggs always had a joke to tell." Gaining his composure, Red tried to change the subject. "How about Frenchie and the others?"

"Frenchie's just fine. He's married with a couple of kids. He's been a financial advisor for most of his adult life. Says he's getting damn near ready for retirement and eager to pack it all in." There was a slight pause. Then Ralph asked, "Hey, do you remember Slick?"

"Sure I do!"

"Well, he told me he owns a Toyota dealership, but you know him; Slick, the consummate bullshitter. For all I know, he could be digging ditches or cleaning septic tanks."

James laughed.

"Slick had a scam going every minute," Ralph relayed.

"He sure did." After a pause, he asked, "Hey! How about Lieutenant Kendall?"

"I spoke to him a few weeks ago. He was devastated about the entire scenario and how that lifer colonel royally screwed Dale. I think his conscience has been bothering him ever since he left 'Nam. You know, Red; he did everything he could including putting Dale in for a decoration and defending it to the hilt. He was simply the low man on an awfully high totem pole. The colonel, with his enormous ego, was an insurmountable asshole."

"That's for sure. But let me ask you. Do you think everyone will complete the affidavits?"

"Without a doubt!"

"That's great," James responded. "What do I do?"

"Tomorrow, I'll send you all the forms by Priority Mail. When you get 'em, fill 'em all out, paying particular attention to the narrative. Remember, the award is based on what's called extraordinary merit and incontestable proof of performance. We know he's a hero. Now we have to persuade the others. Just write a few paragraphs describing what you saw that night, and don't pull any punches. When finished, mail everything to the senator's office. The return address is on the affidavit. The senator's staff will handle it from there."

The conversation between Ralph and James continued for another hour. They talked about the post-war years, their families and anything else they could think about. James asked for the telephone numbers of all the guys. His intention was to call them all in the next few weeks.

Shortly after the call, Ralph thought, *The phone bill is going to be awfully expensive this month*. Then he smiled. The smile was accompanied by a feeling of unbelievable relief as if the weight of the world had suddenly been lifted from his shoulders.

The Pentagon (Hall of Heroes), Washington, D.C.
June 6, 2000
10:10 a.m.

The President was running late. The brief ceremony was scheduled to commence at 10 a.m.

Major Richardson, who was assigned to assist Dale and his family during their stay in the capital region, leaned over and said, "It shouldn't be but another fifteen minutes, Mr. Ives. We've just received confirmation that the President has left the White House. You know, delays like this happen almost all the time. The President gets pulled every which way."

"I understand," Dale responded.

Until a few months ago, Dale could still walk. But since, his illness had progressed so quickly, he was now confined to a wheelchair.

Earlier in the morning, Ralph who had been invited to the ceremony as part of the family, helped Dale dress in the military uniform supplied him by Major Richardson. The jacket comprised all the medals Dale had been awarded while in the military. Ralph was also needed to help Dale maneuver the wheelchair. Due to severe muscle degeneration, Dale needed full-time assistance.

As for immediate family, Dale's wife Sandy and their two children, Mary and Denise were in attendance. Ralph's wife Diane was also present, along with their twenty-two year old son, Charles. Two other relatives had been invited but were unable to attend, one because of illness, the other because of work constraints. The gathering was small.

Dale looked around and felt humbled to be in such honored company. He found it difficult to believe that he, too, would soon be in the distinguished company of so many heroes. Although a revered setting, the alcove was less than spacious. On the walls were framed photographs of previous Medal of Honor winners. In a glass case, several Medals of Honor were displayed on shelves along with a brief text to explain the valorous deeds. The medals were donations from families of deceased recipients.

"The President has arrived," Major Richardson announced to those in attendance. "Mr. Nugent, could you kindly wheel our guest of honor to this position, with his back to the wall," as he pointed to a small area near a podium and microphone.

"My pleasure," Ralph replied. "Is this okay?"

"Perfect," said the major.

Ralph looked down at Dale and as if in a panic said, "For God sake, Dale! Spit out the gum."

Smiling, Dale took it out with his fingers and slid it into the pocket of his jacket.

Ralph looked at Dale with a smirk on his face and exclaimed, "You're disgusting!"

Dale winked back with a devilish look in his eyes.

As the President was walked down the long corridor toward the alcove, Dale looked up at Ralph and made a request: "Help me stand up."

"What? Are you crazy!"

"Yes! I'm crazy!" he replied, with a bit of irritation in his voice. "Now will you help me get to my feet or am I going to have to do this myself? There's no way that I'm going to be sitting in a wheelchair when the President of the United States awards me that medal."

Ralph hesitated as Dale made a feeble attempt to push himself up from the wheelchair before falling back into the seat. Ralph knew he was fighting a losing battle. "All right!" he said. He grabbed Dale with his arms and lifted him up while swinging to his side and holding the dead weight with his left arm securely fastened under Dale's shoulder.

Noticing that his father was having a difficult time holding Dale steady, Ralph's son Charles ran over. "Dad, let me help. I'll hold Uncle Dale up from the other side."

The President had witnessed the entire scene and was genuinely touched. Walking toward Dale through a small crowd of Dale's family and a few Pentagon officials (military and civilian), the President introduced himself to the honored guest. "Corporal Ives," he said, "from what I just observed, I have no doubt you're one of the finest and toughest Marines I've ever met."

"Thank you, Mr. President!" Dale said, saluting as best he could.

The President returned the gesture.

Walking toward the President from the left side were two officers. One held the award citation; the other carried an open display case containing the treasured medal. The first officer stepped to the microphone and read the citation awarded by Congressional authority. The document included all the standard phrases and words: for distinguished gallantry in action . . . with total disregard for his own safety . . . suffering from numerous wounds . . . above and beyond the call of duty . . . conspicuous . . . intrepidity. No mention was ever made, at least directly, of the saving of an enemy soldier, although the citation did allude to Dale's display of humanitarian regard and unselfish acts to his fellow man. Those who knew the entire story realized its meaning and intent. Dale appeared unfazed.

After the citation was read, the second officer stepped forward and stood near the President's side.

"Corporal Ives," the President said trying to disguise his trembling voice. "We are grateful for your valorous deeds. There is no greater honor that our country can bestow upon its military men and women for such heroic service. This belated award should in no way diminish the significance of your bravery and what this medal signifies to the few who are privileged to wear it." The President turned to his side and lifted the medal from its case. Turning toward Dale, he inhaled a deep breath and said, "It is an extreme privilege for me to present to you, Corporal John A. Ives, the Medal of Honor."

Dale lowered his head. The President slipped the blue and white, star-studded ribbon with the suspended five star pendant over Dale's head and rested it around his shirt collar. Adjusting it so to center it on Dale's chest, the President turned around, faced the crowd and said, "May I present to you Corporal John A. Ives, one of fewer than 3,500 military heroes to be awarded our nation's highest award . . . the Medal of Honor."

The small audience clapped enthusiastically. The President stood back and smiled, not wanting to take anything away from the moment.

Dale took it all in. Turning toward the President, he said, "Thank you, Mr. President." The President nodded and continued with his grin. Dale looked out at his family, now beaming with pride. While still standing, Sandy ran over and kissed him. "I love you, honey," she said as tears of joy filled her eyes.

"I love you, too," Dale replied.

Dale's daughters, Mary and Denise, also hurried over, lavishing their father with kisses and hugs.

Still supported by Ralph and Charles, Dale appeared animated as he made a painful attempt to wave at his friends and other dignitaries in attendance.

For a few minutes, a military photographer took photos while the President was shaking Dale's hand. Ralph and Charles were still holding Dale in a standing position but the exuberance of the moment made them forget about the weight they were holding between them.

"Mr. President, I'd like to introduce my family."

Dale not only introduced his wife and daughters, but also Ralph's family as well.

Running late, the President stayed long enough to allow the photographer to take several group photos with the families. He then apologized and said he had some pressing business to attend to. Shaking hands with Dale, he wished him well.

Moments after the President and his entourage disappeared from view down the corridor, Ralph and his son gently guided Dale back down into the wheelchair.

South Hadley, Massachusetts
September 6, 2000
Mid-afternoon to early-evening

After returning home from the award ceremony, Dale's condition worsened. Because of the seriousness of his illness, he had used all his strength by traveling to the Pentagon to accept the belated decoration. Knowing that each day was borrowed time, Dale fought valiantly, perhaps more for his family than himself. He loved them dearly and didn't want them to see him suffer. But he was also a Marine, trained to survive any ordeal. *Never say die* was a legacy he felt committed to uphold.

Three months to the day of Dale's Medal of Honor ceremony, the immediate family was called to his beside. Dale could barely speak. Lying in bed with Sandy sitting at his side, he painfully turned his head toward her. With shallow and labored breathing, Dale said to her, "When I die, promise you'll be strong?"

"I'll try, honey, but I don't want you to leave."

"Sandy," Dale said with a hushed tone, "the Lord will take care of me." He continued, "God willing . . . I'll try to leave you a . . ." but before he could conclude, he lost what little breath that remained in his fragile body. He begin to cough then choke on his own saliva. Turning his head to one side, it took him a few minutes before regaining any semblance of composure, yet he was more strong-minded than ever to relay his message. Again, he looked up at Sandy as he repeated his message, but this time he interjected his speech with pauses to catch his breath and quell his cough. "I'll try . . . to leave you . . . a sign . . . to show . . . I'm at peace."

"That's a tall order, Dale. I don't need a sign, my love."

"Sandy . . . I'll do . . . my best. I promise." Dale muttered.

Sandy gave little thought to his words. She shook her head to acknowledge his remark, before leaning over to give him a kiss on the forehead. Taking Dale's hand, she kissed it and held it firmly against her cheek. "I love you," she said. Her eyes watered.

Dale smiled sheepishly and closed his eyes. Although the medication soothed his pain, he was unable to control his cough. The hack was incessant — dry and frightening. After each cough, Sandy wondered if it would be his last?

Early that evening, Dale lapsed into an irreversible coma. Hours before, the cough fell silent. Dale died but a few hours later — undoubtedly, as he lived — a loving husband, a dedicated father, and most of all, a God-fearing man. After kissing him on the cheek and whispering in his ear, Sandy removed the Bible that was clasped in Dale's left hand — the same Bible that comforted him in Vietnam — when she noticed a dog-eared page. Opening it, she read the marked passage (Psalm 23) out loud. After reading four verses, she could read no more.

The LORD is my shepherd; I shall not want.

He Maketh me to lie down in green pastures: he leadeth me beside the still waters.

He restoreth my soul: he leadeth me in the paths of righteousness for his name's sake.

Yea, though I walk through the valley of the shadow of death, I will fear no evil: for thou art with me; thy rod and thy staff they comfort me . . .

Arlington National Cemetery, Arlington, Virginia
September 12, 2000
Morning

Dale's remains were flown to Ronald Reagan National Airport in Arlington, Virginia, and immediately transported by hearse to a funeral home not far from Arlington National Cemetery. The cemetery, located near the Pentagon, is directly across the Potomac from Washington, D.C. In the waning months, Dale had requested burial there and, as a Medal of Honor recipient, he was entitled to the privilege. Dale knew he would be in good company, resting eternally alongside 268,000 other heroic Americans.

Tuesday, the 12th, was a magnificent day with only a whisper of wind under a cerulean sky. The temperature was a comfortable 80 degrees.

The funeral was held at 8:30 a.m. in a small chapel in a congested end of the city. The mass and eulogies lasted less than an hour. The funeral procession to Arlington would take but twenty minutes.

Upon arrival at the main entrance, six Marines transferred the coffin to a caisson hitched to a team of six black horses. Marching toward the gravesite on a narrow paved road, the horse-drawn carriage lumbered up a slight incline before coming to an abrupt halt near a freshly dug grave. Seated in a black stretch limousine directly behind the caisson were the surviving members of the Ives family. Three other limos, all with lights turned on, completed the entourage.

The Marine honor guards escorting the remains guardedly lifted the flag-draped coffin from the platform. In short-stepped cadence, they carried the coffin to the gravesite before positioning it over the vault. On command, they gracefully laid the casket down on the wide green canvas and nylon strapping. Only then were the immediate family and invited guests allowed to gather around the coffin.

The ceremony was reverent, yet brief. A Marine Corps chaplain, Captain Marsh, presided over the graveside service prior to the body being interred.

Taking hold of the flag draped over the coffin, the Marines meticulously began folding the flag taking precautions to prevent the colors from touching the ground. Only two honor guards performed the finishing folds into the symbolic tri-cornered shape. Holding the flag waist high and facing Sandy, the lead Marine in the detail presented it to the widow as he said, "On behalf of the President of the United States, the Commandant of the Marine Corps, and a grateful nation, please accept this flag as a symbol of our appreciation for your loved one's service to Country and Corps. God bless you and this family, and God bless the United States of America."

Accepting the tribute, she kissed the flag and placed it under her arm. Sandy took a few short steps forward and laid a dozen white long-stemmed roses on the lid of the coffin before stepping back. Mary and Denise followed suit, each placing a white rose upon the coffin. Behind Sandy stood Ralph and Diane. In the background, under the shade of an oak tree not far from the grieving family, stood four gray-haired gentlemen: Kendall, LeBeau, McElroy, and Vendetti. LeBeau supported himself with a cane. Making the somber trek from different parts of the country, they came as veterans to pay their final respects to a fellow comrade-in-arms, a friend, and a highly decorated and well-deserving war hero.

After completing a prayer, Chaplain Marsh sprinkled holy water on the casket. As he leaned over the coffin, he tossed a small amount of dirt while reciting a brief biblical verse from Ecclesiastes 3:20: "All go unto one place; all are of the dust, and all turn to dust again."

Before the ceremony concluded, a Marine from the detail walked over and stood next to the coffin. Briskly saluting the remains, he turned and stepped toward a monument that, up until the present, had been covered. Lifting the gray veil that concealed the plain marble stone, the inscription was now visible for all to read:

John D. Ives
August 16, 1948 - September 6, 2000
Medal of Honor
Republic of South Vietnam
September 26, 1967

Engraved on the back, right-hand corner of the stone were two small letters, *PH*, signifying the award of the Purple Heart.

Nearby, a seven-man firing squad stood at attention. The head of the detail commanded: "Ready!" as each man loaded a blank round in the rifle chamber and unlocked the safety lever. "Aim!" all lifted their M-14 rifles and angled them toward the sky. *"Fire!"* The seven-round volley resonated for a brief second. The identical command was given twice more in final salute.

On a small, grassy knoll overlooking the burial plot, a Marine bugler played *Taps*. The melancholy notes echoed throughout the cemetery. Respecting the occasion, visitors and cemetery laborers at other gravesites stopped what they were doing until the bugler concluded his call.

As the casket was lowered into the vault, Sandy clutched the flag tightly against her breast. Tears welled in her eyes. For support, her children held her firmly under each arm, but Sandy remembered her promise to Dale. She stood tall and remained strong.

Ralph Nugent looked up to the heavens, completely oblivious to his surroundings. His eyes became bleary. In a voice choked with emotion, he said out loud, "I love you, brother . . . may you rest in peace!" No longer able to control his feelings, he broke down and cried. Diane lightly patted him on the arm.

Sandy, maintaining remarkable composure and upholding the final promise to her husband, looked in Ralph's direction. Clutching the flag in her right hand, she stepped toward him and gently placed her arms around his shoulders. Trying to console him, she whispered in his ear, "We all loved him, Ralph!"

With Sandy still hugging him, Ralph gradually regained his composure. Pulling back but not breaking the embrace, he said, "Sandy, I'm awfully sorry. I guess I've been holding it in for too long."

"I understand. You and Dale were just like brothers."

"That we were!" he said as he wiped away the remaining tears that ran down his cheeks.

As Diane walked with their son back to the car, Ralph escorted Sandy and her daughters to the waiting limo.

Denise was first to notice what appeared to be small pieces of paper cascading down the hillside, rising off the ground a few feet then tumbling and twisting over and over in the grass, only to rise again. One of the objects reflected the bright glare of the sun as if someone was shining a flashlight directly in her eyes. She stopped abruptly causing the others behind her to do the same. In any other circumstance, no one would have noticed, but Denise thought it odd. Though leaves were strewn on the ground, only the paper

165

The Mysterious Gum Wrapper

was caught in the updraft. "Look at that!" she uttered while pointing at the objects. Everyone stared, mesmerized by the strange phenomena.

Sandy sensed it was headed in her direction. Suddenly, the breeze lessened and the papers dropped to the ground, coming to rest near her feet. Reaching down, she picked them up. "Oh my God!" she exclaimed, while covering her mouth.

"What is it?" Denise asked.

"It's a wrapper and foil . . . from a stick of gum." Hesitating momentarily, Sandy caught her breath. "It's *Juicy Fruit*!" she exclaimed in exultation. "It's his favorite flavor . . . Dale's!" as she held them up like an honored trophy for all to see.

"Ralph! Could you hold the flag for a second, please?"

"Of course," he said, taking it from Sandy's grip.

With great care, she placed the wrapper and foil in one of the sleeves of her pocketbook. Glancing up at the sky, she stood transfixed for a second or two before gracefully lowering her head. Turning toward her daughters, she said, "Your father has just received his highest award — eternal life with the Almighty. No mortal can ever take that away."

The girls tried to understand, but found it difficult. Denise spoke first. "Do you really think Dad had ..."

Sandy interrupted. "Yes . . . yes I do!"

Grabbing her daughters firmly by the hand, Sandy looked at each of them and said, "Girls! I feel so much better now. I think it's best we go home."

THE YOUNG BOY

No young man believes he shall ever die.
-William Hazlitt, *On the Feeling of Immortality of Youth
in Literary Remains* (1936)

The early July afternoon was breathtaking. Although cumulus clouds appeared in the sky, few blocked the radiant sun during their passing. Earlier in the day the wind was breezy but within the last hour had subsided with barely a hint of breeze. Temperatures hovered in the low eighties. It was Saturday, the 4th — Independence Day. The time: 1 p.m.

Residents of the small town began to gather. Many arrived early to stake their claim for the most advantageous spot to view the parade, an event scheduled to commence an hour later. Some came to be entertained; others to show support for their local heroes — World War II and Korean War veterans. On Thursday, details of the day's events were published on the front-page of the town's weekly newspaper, but only a two-sentence blurb appeared in Friday's regional edition of the metropolitan newspaper.

The parade route was less than picturesque. On one side of the road stood three-story tenement houses in various stages of disrepair and on the other, a rocky ravine the remnant of a failed right-of-way of a long-since defunct railroad. Scrub bushes of varying height were scattered throughout the chasm. The property appeared abandoned. Distracting further from the view, lazy and thoughtless inhabitants used the area as a refuse heap. Discarded beer cans and items as large as washing machines could be seen if anyone was willing to approach and look down the steep embankment. As if it couldn't get uglier, towering electric poles carried high tension wires, north and south, over the road and far off into the distance. Had the parade been a typical Fourth of July celebration, it would have been scheduled, as it had been in previous years, for the downtown shopping area of the quaint New England community. But for this event, location was the important determinant — the corner of Mill Lane and Walnut Street.

At precisely 2:15 p.m., a young boy about twelve arrived on his prized possession: a Raleigh English Racer — a sleek-looking bicycle with slender, twenty-six inch wheels. Dressed in blue jeans, white tee-shirt, black canvas sneakers and a baseball cap with the letter 'M' embroidered on the front, there was little that set him apart from the others. Except for a black eye suffered after misjudging a fly ball in a Little League Baseball game, he easily blended in with the crowd.

Earlier in the morning, the boy's father told him about the parade. "Lucas. You should go," the father said. "Your uncles will be marching."

Having nothing better to do and because the event was close to home, Luke made the decision. Pedaling his bicycle a short distance up a steep paved road, he turned right and sped a mile or two before reaching his destination. He was hardly winded. Leaving his bicycle lying in the gutter, Luke raced toward the crowd. Luckily, he arrived in the nick of time. Standing in the middle of the road, he watched as the military contingent marched toward him. The first division consisted of middle-aged veterans. As the men approached, he recognized two of his uncles. Both were in the front row. They wore beige military uniforms with the bottom half of their narrow black ties tucked securely between the buttonholes of their shirts. Their pants were folded neatly into their boots and partially covered by laced, white leggings. The men looked proud and marched with an air of invincibility. Each shouldered a Browning automatic rifle. Medals and decorations they'd earned during the war were pinned to their shirt pockets. The silver and bronze medallions caught the young boy's eyes as they sparkled in the midday sun. Luke could hardly take his eyes off them.

Standing transfixed, Luke happened to notice one of the flag bearers. Another uncle — not a soldier but a sailor dressed in white — carried an American flag that rippled gloriously in the light afternoon breeze. Spectators lining the street waved miniature flags and applauded. Some were moved to tears.

Within yards of where the boy stood, the column veered left onto a narrow street. In less than a minute, the parade came to an abrupt halt.

The event was planned to serve a dual purpose. A memorial square was to be dedicated in memory of a fallen soldier who gave his last full measure during World War II. Celebrating the Fourth and dedicating the square on the same day seemed right and honorable.

Surprisingly, the ceremony lasted a short while. A priest consecrated the monument, and a town dignitary made a few appropriate remarks. "In my capacity as Selectman from the town of Ridgefield, I dedicate this site as Reilly's Square in memory of Joseph P. Reilly, killed in action while nobly serving his country," he concluded. The surviving parents were presented a citation. Soon after, a rifle squad fired a twenty-one-gun salute. As to be expected, youngsters dove for the empty shell casings as if treasure. Luke was no exception. Though hot to the touch, he filled his pockets with the spent cartridges. Minutes later, he jumped on his bike and rode home.

Luke was affected by what he saw, although it would take years before he grasped the true meaning of the day.
The event wasn't an especially momentous occasion. For those present — adults and children alike — the sentiments of the day faded quickly. Within weeks nearly everyone in the town had forgotten; except for Luke. The vision of the marching veterans, especially his uncles and the medals they wore, was now indelibly etched in his mind. Sadly, it was not for the right reason.
Years passed. Luke became a teenager, then a young man. No longer were townspeople talking about World War II or the somewhere in Southeast Asia. Few had ever heard of the place.

As his uncles before him, Luke was drafted into the Armed Forces and called upon to fight in a faraway land. With the grace of God, he, too, survived the ordeal. His homecoming, however, was different, far different. There were no marching bands, parades or flag-waving spectators. For decades, no one asked, "What was it like?" Even as a young veteran among older veterans, he felt an outcast. Luke's return was bittersweet.

The Elder Statesman

The mental grime of serving in Vietnam would take years before it would wash away. In the ensuing years, Luke grew into an adult, but never once did he lose his hard-earned pride. He knew, all too well, about the hardships of war while accomplishing his assigned duties and responsibilities to the best of his ability. As days turned to months and months into years, Luke never failed to reflect upon what had inspired him during his days in combat and now as a veteran: watching his proud and gallant uncles marching in the hometown parade. Only now, he understood so much more.

Four months after returning from Vietnam, Lucas Teasdale married his high school sweetheart, Missy. In less than a year, they had a son. Jonathan was only a few months shy of his seventeenth birthday when he was killed in a terrible accident after joy-riding in the family car. Luke and Missy were devastated. In the issuing years, Luke's less than auspicious adventures took more unexpected dips, vexing twists and hair-pin turns than an award-winning coaster ride; yet, miraculously, in spite of numerous transgressions — and there were scores — he managed to skirt the law.

Missy never gave up hope. It wasn't until Luke sought counseling and finally came to grips with his past (Vietnam and the loss of his son) that his life and Missy's changed for the better.

The driveway was already jam-packed with cars when the green VW convertible pulled into the yard.

"Just park it on the lawn," Vinny said to the late arrivals. "Ya, that's fine. Just leave it right there." Vinny and his wife, Martha, didn't expect such a large turnout for their son's going away party.

Smiling, Vinny walked over to the car and offered his greetings to the occupants. "Thanks for coming. It's great to see you both again. How long was the drive?"

"About three hours," Missy said. "It was easy. Thank God it's Saturday."

Vinny shook hands with his brother, Luke, and kissed his sister-in-law even before they got out of the car. "I'm so happy to have you join in the festivities," Vinny said, "even though I wish it was . . ."

Luke interjected. "Vinny, if you don't mind, I'd like to have a few minutes alone with Jeb before I leave today."

"I was hoping you'd say somethin' to him, Luke," Vinny said, sounding relieved. "Martha and I talked about that last night. Jeb's so gung-ho, we're afraid he's going to do somethin' foolish and put his life in jeopardy."

Luke looked at his younger brother. "It's a normal reaction, Vinny. Remember, how I was before I left for 'Nam. Even after dad talked to me about our uncles in World War II, it never, really, hit home."

"That's for sure," Vinny said.

Luke continued: "I tried to understand, Vinny, but I was young and naive. I guess I though I was indestructible. I didn't get the message until just before I had to get on that plane in Okinawa." Luke flinched. "Give me some time with Jeb," Luke requested, "and let me see what I can do. Okay, Vinny?"

"Thanks, Luke. Martha and I really appreciate it."

The party lasted several hours. Late in the evening, after talking to a few guests, Jeb walked out of the house onto the back porch. There, he ran into his uncle coming up the stairs. "Uncle Luke," Jeb said. "Before I forget, I'd like to thank you and Aunt Missy for coming today."

"Jeb," Luke said. "I had to come."

"Well, I'm glad you did," Jeb responded.

"No. You don't understand. I really did have to come. I wanted to talk to you about a few things."

Jeb had an inkling of what was to be discussed and wished it didn't have to be. It was a difficult subject, and he knew it. There wasn't much he could say.

Putting his arm around Jeb's shoulder, Luke looked at his nephew and said, "It's nothin' like you could ever imagine, Jeb. There's no glory; absolutely, no glory whatsoever."

"I know, Uncle Luke."

"I know you think you know, Jeb, but there's no military training in the world, at least that I know of, that can prepare you for what you're about to experience." Luke paused. "When I was a young boy, I watched my uncles march in a parade . . . right here in Ridgefield. They were veterans of World War II. At the time, the medals they had pinned to their uniforms impressed the hell out of me. Little did I know, the medals were nothing more than window dressing. Jeb, I came home with many of the same medals. They're now sitting in the back of my dresser drawer. I can't tell you the last time I looked at them." Luke waited for a reaction, but Jeb stood expression-less. "Now, I'm not sayin' you can't be proud. You should be. I'm just tellin' you to watch yourself. Understand?"

"I think so, Uncle Luke."

"Jeb," Luke said. "I lost my only child, several years ago. Besides your Aunt Missy, and your mother and father, you are one of the few things in my life that I really care about. I don't want to lose you; neither does your mom and dad."

"I'll be careful, Uncle Luke, I promise."

"I know you will, Jeb. Remember: everyone wants you to come home safe and sound."

"I will, Uncle Luke."

Just as Jeb acknowledged his uncle's comments, Missy walked toward them. Seeing his wife at the bottom of the stairs, Luke hastily reach into his pocket, pulled out a highly-polished silver dollar and handed it to Jeb. "Here, put this in your pocket."

"Gee, thanks, Uncle Luke," Jeb said.

"Now, Jeb. I want you to carry it with you to Iraq. It will bring you good luck."

"Thanks again, Uncle Luke. I promise…I'll always keep it with me."

Just as Missy approached, Luke turned away from his nephew. Without saying goodbye, he put his head down and slowly walked away. With Missy at his side, Luke broke down and sobbed, covering his face with his hands. Jeb knew what was happening but was uncertain how to react. It was the first time he saw a grown man cry. Suddenly, his heart became heavy, and a lump appeared in his throat. Not knowing what else to do, he yelled from the porch, "I love you, Uncle Luke."

Raising his arm, Luke acknowledged the comment and waved. He never looked back.

ABOUT THE AUTHOR

Born and raised in Massachusetts, Frank Grzyb graduated with a bachelor's degree from Nichols College. Shortly thereafter, he received an MBA from Farleigh Dickinson University. With the war raging in Vietnam, Frank was drafted into the Army. After completing basic training, he was assigned to the Army Infantry School at Ft. Benning, Georgia. A year later, he was sent to Vietnam. During his tour, Frank was awarded several decorations, most notably a Bronze Star, Purple Heart, and Army Commendation Medal. His first book, *Touch by the Dragon*, is a critically acclaimed collection of gripping war narratives. Reissued in trade paperback as *A Story for All Americans*, the book includes a telling introduction by U.S. Senator John F. Kerry. Frank has contributed numerous articles to newspapers, historical magazines, and literary journals. Recently retired after working some twenty years as a Personnel Management Advisor at a Naval research and development laboratory, Frank is currently pursuing his dream: the craft of writing. Frank Grzyb and his family currently reside in Rhode Island.

ABOUT THE ILLUSTRATOR

Alexandre V. Kouznetsov, better known as Sasha, hails from the Ukraine. As a young man, Sasha graduated from the prestigious College of Graphic Design in Kiev. Before coming to America, he served in the elite Special Forces of the Russian Army. For nearly a decade, Sasha has worked as the artist-in-residence at a preservation society in Rhode Island. Here he continues to refine his multi-faceted skills as a talented artist and graphic designer. Over the years, Sasha has illustrated books written in both Russian and English. Strongly influenced by the likes of El Greco, Vermeer, Vrubel, and Dali, Kouznetsov's work is haunting, yet passionate and exhilarating.

ACRONYMS

AK-47	Enemy assault rifle
ARVN	Army of the Republic of South Vietnam
AWOL	Absent without leave
Bush	The jungle, wilderness, or enemy territory
Charlie	A Viet Cong soldier
Cherry	A new replacement soldier
DEROS	Date eligible for return from overseas
FNG	Fuckin' New Guy: A derogatory term used to identify a new replacement
Gook	Derogatory name given to anyone of Asian ancestry
Hootch	A native hut
LZ	Landing zone
M-16 A1	American infantry assault rifle
Medevac	Medical evacuation by plane or helicopter
MPC	Military payment certificate
Native Sport	Patrolling for the enemy
Nuoc-mum	A pungent fish sauce used to flavor rice
NVA	North Vietnamese Army
Point	The lead position in a platoon and usually the most dangerous because of direct exposure to the enemy
PX	Post Exchange
RTO	Radio telephone operator
Sappers	Enemy demolition soldiers
VC	Viet Cong

.